I0714378

THE SNIPER'S PRAYER

The Art Of Prayer, Prayers That Get Result

DR. ENAHORO FRANCIS OVIENMHADA

Copyright @2021 by Dr. Enahoro Francis Ovienmhada

This publication contains the opinions and ideas of its author. It is intended to provide helpful and informative material on the subjects addressed in the publication. The author and publisher specifically disclaim all responsibility for any liability, loss or risk, personal or otherwise, which is incurred as a consequence, directly or indirectly, of the use and application of any of the contents of this book.

WORKBOOK PRESS LLC
187 E Warm Springs Rd,
Suite B285, Las Vegas, NV 89119, USA

Website: https://workbookpress.com/
Hotline: 1-888-818-4856
Email: admin@workbookpress.com

Ordering Information:
Quantity sales. Special discounts are available on quantity purchases by corporations, associations, and others.
For details, contact the publisher at the address above.

ISBN-13:   978-1-954753-07-5 (Paperback Version)
              978-1-953839-90-9 (Digital Version)

REV. DATE: 26/01/2021

DEDICATION

I dedicate this book to my wife, Dr. Agnes Ovienmhada, who has been a rock of support to the Ministry. I also dedicate the book to our son, Sharon-David Irebhose Ovienmhada, our only child who was born out of a "Sniper's Prayer." To Edene and our grandchildren, Zion, Benaiah, Abishai and Eleazar (David's mighty men). May the Joshua generation arise, possess their land and enter into God's rest.

THE COMMISSION

"I have called you to be like unto Moses, to call out a people."

"There remaineth therefore a rest to the people of God." Hebrews 4:9

"Let us therefore fear, lest, a promise being left us of entering into his rest, any of you should seem to come short of it." Hebrews 4:1

"For the earnest expectation of the creature waiteth for the manifestation of the sons of God." Romans 8:19

"You will never know who you are until you know who God is."

Dr. Enahoro Francis Ovienmhada

FOREWORD

The Sniper's Prayer by my dear friend, Apostle Enahoro Francis Ovienmhada is destined to become a spiritual classic in the same order of Christian classics such as Andrew Murray's *With Christ in the School of Prayer* or E.M Bounds' *The Power of Prayer*. In this life-changing book, Apostle Francis endeavors to show the great similarities between the Snipers in the military and God's militant army, which is His Church. The Church is His governing body in the earth. Apostle Francis uses a confederacy of spiritual and natural parallels to demonstrate the efficacy of this powerful revelation and demonstrate that Christians all over the world can be trained to effectively pray at a whole new level. *The Sniper's Prayer* is not a book for spiritual babies who want to live on the milk of the word of God. It is a prayer book designed for those who are hungry for more of God and those who want to carry God's governmental power and authority into this world. I highly recommend this book for anybody who is serious about knowing Jesus and experiencing His supernatural power in our 21st-century. Books such as these come once in a lifetime because it takes that long for God to create vessels that He can use to demonstrate the realities of what is in this book, men and women of God such as Apostle Francis. I highly recommend that you read this book while fasting or in exclusion when you are spending time with the Lord. I have no doubt Satan, fearing the spiritual potency of this book, will try to distract you. Don't let him!

Yours for His Kingdom,
Dr. Francis Myles
Bestselling Author, *Issuing Divine Restraining Orders from the Courts of Heaven*

PREFACE

A long time ago, I watched a movie titled, *The Enemy at the Gate*. It was about a Russian Sniper named Vasily Grigoryevich Zaytsev, who terrorized the Germans. The Germans sent their best Sniper for a face-off with the Russian Sniper. The movie began with the young Russian Sniper taking instructions from his father on how to kill foxes. As I continued to watch the movie, I began to imagine how people perfect the work related to their profession and I wondered if we could not apply the same principles to kingdom activities.

Today, men have developed cruise missiles that are programmed to hit their targets thousands of miles away. The scripture declares:

"So shall my word be that goeth forth out of my mouth: it shall not return unto me void, but it shall accomplish that which I please, and it shall prosper in the thing whereto I sent it." Isaiah 55:11.

It takes a skilled marksman to hit his target, even 80% of the time. Here, we have a one hundred percent hit all the time.

The Day of the Jackal was another movie I watched many years ago.
The Sniper was so confident in his ability, that he went with only one bullet. I began to search for Snipers in the Bible and to identify the qualities and character of a Sniper.

"Among all this people there were seven hundred chosen men left-

handed; every one could sling stones at an hair breadth, and not miss." Judges 20:16

I read of David's mighty men and their exploits. These were supermen. I looked at Jesus, the greatest Sniper of all time. His word never failed. I was amazed at what the Scriptures said concerning Samuel:

"And Samuel grew, and the LORD was with him, and did let none of his words fall to the ground." 1 Samuel 3:19

The exploits of David were outstanding. He was great with the sling.

"And David put his hand in his bag, and took thence a stone, and slang it, and smote the Philistine in his forehead, that the stone sunk into his forehead; and he fell upon his face to the earth." 1 Samuel 17:49

I began to ask myself, "Who are the anointed ones at the end time,
men who will do exploits?" I found out that Jesus spoke of, "He that overcometh." Jesus goes on to state very clearly that "The works that I do shall ye do and greater works than these." My heart was aflame to write this book to inspire men to become God's Snipers at the end of this age. The age-old face-off with the enemy is coming to a head. God is putting in place His anointed ones who will be more than a match for their enemies.

May God inspire and motivate the readers of this book to overcome in the Name of Jesus Christ, Amen.

"And there arose not a prophet since in Israel like unto Moses, whom the LORD knew face to face; In all the signs and the wonders, which the LORD sent him to do in the land of Egypt to Pharaoh,

and to all his servants, and to all his land; And in all that mighty hand and in all the great terror which Moses shewed in the sight of all Israel."
Deuteronomy 34:10-12

My prayer is…Lord, do it again!!!

SECOND PREFACE

This book has been sitting idle on my computer for about 14 years. Recently, a lady bought one of my books titled, *Healing!!! The Children's Bread* and was blessed by it. She then asked if I could mentor her. She also asked if I had published other books. I told her I had published three books but that two were out of print with fourteen other books which are yet to be published. I decided to send her *Let It Rain*, my second published book and this book, *The Sniper's Prayer*, to which I have added two new chapters titled The Key of David and The Menace Of The Prophetic Hounds, in light of current events. She started reading *The Sniper's Prayer* and asked why I had not yet published it. I decided to read it again and I could not drop it. I began to wonder myself why I had not yet published it. I guess it is procrastination or it could be that God's appointed time had not yet come.

In recent years, I have watched *The American Sniper*. It is the story of America's deadliest Sniper, Chris Kyle, a Navy SEAL, who was killed not in the tour of duty but here at home. PTSD has become the scourge of many American soldiers. I know God has the answer to PTSD and people who are traumatized should seek God.

Recently I researched out the world's deadliest Sniper nicknamed "The White Death," a Finish farmer by the name of Simo Hayha, who terrorized the Russian Red Army and was so named.

In Nigeria, so many decades ago, there was an advertisement by a bank that read "Wise men bank with ....." The female gender did not really like it and they had to add "and women, too." Now that I must publish this book, it is imperative to acknowledge "Lady Death," the Russian female Sniper, Lyudila Pavlichenko, also Klavdiya Kalugina. When I tried researching American female Snipers, there was nothing to go on except that Jennifer Donaldson, nicknamed "G.I Jane," was the first female graduate of the National Guard Sniper School in 2001.

However, I salute our brave and heroic American women that have distinguished themselves in the various military services.

My sermon *Leprosy In The House* (Leviticus 14:34-45), in Chapter 10, unfortunately has had it's fulfillment and seven families who were offended at my sermon and did not take heed are now divorced.

Now, this book is about prayers and my prayer is that praying men and women will arise as the age long battle with darkness is coming to a close. It is said of Bloody Mary, Queen of Scotland, "I fear the prayers of John Knox more than all the assembled armies of Europe." John Knox, a man of prayer said, "Give me Scotland, or I die."

Where are the men and women of prayer that would affect nations?

Where are the Praying Hydes? Where are the Father Nashes of our time?

Yehovah, change our lives and use us for your glory, is my cry.

May this timely book provoke you in Jesus' name, Amen!

Acknowledgments

The Apostle Paul rightly said "I can do all things through Christ who strengthens me." Grace was poured upon me to write this book.

I would also like to thank my wife for understanding the need for my time away physically, mentally and emotionally, while writing this book. To my brother Michael Ovienmhada for editing this book and the ever so resourceful Kimberly Sparrow for checking out all the scripture references in this book. YeHoVaH richly bless them.

THE PURPOSE OF THIS BOOK

The purpose of this writing is to awaken the real man in us. The new birth is the birth of the spirit man, God's battle axe. It is only with the spirit man that we can reclaim all that Adam lost. Our spirit man is the dwelling place of God; it is the place where God is enthroned and like Paul the Apostle rightly said, *"In Him I live in Him I move in Him I have my being."* Paul did not stop there. He concluded, *"I live by the faith of the Son of God"* – The God kind of faith. A word spoken in the spirit as opposed to those spoken in the flesh shall not be void of effect but shall perform that for which it has been sent. It is the revelation of the word of God. Paul used Mt. Sinai as an allegory. I have done the same using the Sniper as an allegory of the spirit man. It is about learning the art of prayer; prayers that get results. It is about training the spirit man and feeding the spirit man. This book is about God's Supermen or Oracles in this last age whose words will not fail nor fall to the ground. This book declares the counsel of God and it has nothing to do with your feelings. It is a message that will make the heart glad for those who are tired of the words of men. It is about hitting the bull's eye 100% of the time. I offer this book to every discerning heart who wants God's utmost. As you read, expect miracles to happen to you, for you and through you.

ENDORSEMENTS

In *The Sniper's Prayer*, Dr. Francis Ovienmhada brilliantly draws a detailed comparison between the strategic ministry of prayer and the work of a military Sniper. With the incorruptible word of God in our hearts as ammunition, bullets of salvation, healing and deliverance are released from our lips when we boldly pray, prophesy and proclaim the living word of God. What will the result look like? When our words hit the bull's eye, we witness the salvation of the lost, deliverance for the captives, healing for the sick and prosperity for the impoverished. I strongly encourage you to read and practice the contents of this thought-provoking book on strategic prayer. I highly recommend it!

Robert J. Winters, DMin
Senior Pastor
Prepare the Way International Church
Phoenix, AZ

It is my privilege to recommend this anointed revelation, *The Sniper's Prayer*, a very timely book written on the true spiritual qualities of overcoming men and women of God in this time of anarchy and unrest. It presents solid spiritual warfare revelations so desperately needed in the Church today.

I have known Apostle Francis Ovienmhada for over a decade and have labored with him in the evangelistic fields of Nigeria, Ghana and here in the USA.

Michael W. Smith, M.S., C.R.C., C.D.M.S./R.
Professional Counselor
Arizona Deliverance Center
HardcoreChristianity.Com

I have known the author since 2004 when we first met in a rather dramatic prophetic encounter in the late summer of that year. The Lord had me call out his Apostolic/Prophetic role in the end-time Church of God. I have watched this simple, meek and audacious prophet of God with much interest since then and I am exceedingly glad that the man and his message have remained consistent.

Reading through the book, I am confident that God has given His servant a timely message to a Church immersed in identity crises. In one of my books on warfare, I noted that we are in a time of complete turmoil, globally. Today, all around us and all over the world, we hear the battle cry in all spheres of human endeavor. As Jesus predicted, nations are rising against nations in war; the drumbeat of war is everywhere.

There is religious, political and socioeconomic turmoil like we have
never seen before all over the world and, naturally, the hearts of many are failing for fear. Strong nations like the United States and Russia are increasing their military budgets to prepare for the unknown. There is something in the air and the outlook is bad and ominous. What a good time to prepare to fill our roles for what lies ahead.

In this book, the first in a series, Apostle Francis is being used by God to sound the battle cry for the anointed army to strap on their boots and prepare adequately and effectively for spiritual warfare. God is calling His army to train and prepare to be sharpshooters. Apostle Francis, a tested war General in God's army, is sounding a wake-up call to the Church to prepare a people ready for the Lord of hosts. The book, *The Sniper's Prayer*, is written to prepare an army of people who, like the Navy SEALs of the US Army can endure the ruggedness of rigorous combat training and then deploy into the spiritually dark places of the earth, ready to be spiritually specific, accurate and on target sharpshooters for God's kingdom. This book is a must read for all who are prepared to move on with God and embrace the next level revival and authentic prophetic move on the earth. I wholeheartedly recommend it to be used in Prayer Schools, Bible Institutes and as a training manual for the emerging end-time army of the Lord, everywhere. I wish everyone an impactful reading. I recommend *The Sniper's Prayer*.

Apostle Patrick Odigie
Prophetic Power House Ministries
New York & Virginia, USA

It was William Shakespeare who said in, *As You Like It*, "All the world's a stage, And all the men and women merely players." Shakespeare may not have been born again, yet he was echoing a kingdom truth that is hidden to many or rather a truth that many see but don't rate as important in the things of God's kingdom. This, however, is a truth that has dire consequences for all who will disregard it. They may end up becoming like the wicked servant who never used the talent he was given. (Luke 19:11-27).

What acts made one servant to profit and another to be unprofitable are matters that should engage the mind of a serious minded Christian. Unfortunately, many that come into the commonwealth of the faith of true disciples of Christ don't know what they are in for. The preaching of "gain" as proof of approval by Christ has brought in a motley crowd with myopic understanding of the faith. The walk into the knowledge of the purpose of their calling that brings God pleasure eludes such people. And that is what is responsible for the mediocre and moribund status of many Christians today.

In *The Sniper's Prayer*, Apostle Francis Ovienmhada has sought to make clear to Christians, through allegories and analogies, that beyond being born again, there is the opportunity to be called and trained into a special class of Christians, God's elite corps. Using the existence of such a group in the military, drawn exclusively from special squads like Navy SEALs, the Army Green Berets and Marines, all of whom are trained to disrupt the supply chains, decimate the command structures and generally discomfit the enemy, he casts God's Snipers in this imagery.

Quoting him, *"A Sniper in the spiritual context is a person anointed to pull down principalities and powers, rulers of darkness and wicked spirits in the heavenlies. A Sniper is anointed to eliminate satanic agents in their different facets (religious, government or individuals) of existence and operations through the efficacy of prayers that cannot fail."* Their characteristics and their rigorous training by God are well laid out for any Christian to assimilate and desire to partake of.

Citing numerous examples from the Bible that we may not so recognize, such as the 700 left-handed children of Benjamin who never missed their targets (Judges 20:16); the sons of Issachar who understood the times and gave Israel directions (1 Chr. 12:32); David's special men and the likes of Samuel, Nehemiah, Moses, Zerubabel, these men served Israel (God) specially to protect and liberate God's people.

Stating that although time may be different, the setting in this age is the same; people need to be delivered and saved from the stranglehold of Satan. Every true believer is a part of God's corps to be Snipers as kings, priests and prophets (I Peter 2:9; Rev. 1:6, I Peter 4:11; Isaiah 61:1-6).

The question is, who is functioning in these graces? Not many! That is why this book is a must read for all, young or old believers. Today, we see churches full, cars carrying Christianity related stickers and smile with such quotes as "We are Winning the Battle Against the Devil." Apostle Francis, through this book as one who has walked the path of victorious engagement over the powers of darkness, bringing many out of the bondage of Satan, is challenging you to ascertain whether you fit into this corps but more than that, he is encouraging you to take steps to attain the same. Be a Sniper for God. I end with a quote by Samuel Insull, "Aim for the top! There's plenty of room there. There are so few at the top, it's almost lonely."

Pastor Afolabi Oladele
The Brethren Church
Lagos, Nigeria.

Get this Book!!

Frankie is my older brother. We grew up together and went to the same schools and slept in the same room, sharing a bed for many years growing up. I testify to the truthfulness and dedication of Frankie to the ministry. His walk with God began when we were yet children. Hear what he has to say. He does not need your money. If he gets it, he gives it to the poor. He feeds the Sheep. Was that not what Jesus instructed Peter to do to show his love for him?

Michael O. Ovienmhada
Proud to be his younger brother

Contributing to this book, *The Sniper's Prayer*, is a miracle for a lost but found sister like me. I lost contact with Rev. Francis over 28 years ago. Thanks to Facebook, we recently reconnected. Reading through this amazing book is indeed a great privilege for me. I have known Rev. Enahoro Francis Ovienmhada and his family for 33 years and as a young adult then, I have never seen a soul so committed to populating the kingdom of God and depopulating hell in the same measure. Indeed, he is a Sniper. My siblings and I are living testimonies of how he committed his time, treasure and talent to direct our footsteps technically and wisely to Jesus Christ. He would drive over 70 kilometers to our residence in another town on Sunday morning to pick us up for service. He taught us commitment, faith and perseverance. He practically adopted us, supplying our needs and shielding us from the apparent danger of temptation. Reading through *The Sniper's Prayer*, with the supporting scriptures therein, I concluded that Rev. Francis wrote out the heart of God with regards to the purpose of God for our lives. He instructed us how we are to put on the whole armor of God, particularly in prayers, so that we can dislodge the scheming of the devil and his cohorts.

I must say I witnessed some of the instances mentioned in this book. I watched several years back, how a very determined big brother; Enahoro, through prayers of faith healed the sick, made a barren woman receive her miracle baby, overcame lack and wants while using every opportunity to minister to souls. His ever-helpful wife, Dr. Agnes, is a wonderful, tolerant wife who was always available to help. While he strives to make the perfect mark, his life has been an inspiration to all of us. He is truly a Sniper for the Lord, an end time soldier of the LORD of Hosts. What Rev. Francis has written in this all-important book is a must read for all Christians striving to make his/her heavenly journey.

It's not an easy road but with the guidance of the Holy Spirit and the wisdom imparted in this book, victory is sure with Jesus on our side. I recommend this book to every believer. I graciously endorse this wonderful spiritual manual, *The Sniper's Prayer*.

Prof. Olubukola Monisola Oyawoye
Dean, Faculty of science,
Adeleke University
Ede, Oshun State, Nigeria.

Contents

Chapter 1
  Who is a Sniper? 27
Chapter 2
  The Holy Ghost Invasion Corp Sniper's School 32
Chapter 3
  A Sniper's Prayer 37
Chapter 4
  The Spirit of Cain 58
Chapter 5
  It Takes a Sniper 62
Chapter 6
  The Trigger 69
Chapter 7
  A Man of Violence 75
Chapter 8
  The Perfect Sniper 84
Chapter 9
  Lessons in Prayer 89
Chapter 10
  Manifestation of the Sons of God 106
Chapter 11
  Prayerlessness 124
Chapter 12
  Hitting the Bull's Eye 126
Chapter 13
  The Eyes of a Sniper 149
Chapter 14
  God's Special Forces 153
Chapter 15
  Prayers In the Bible 161
Chapter 16
  The Menace Of The Prophetic Hounds 166
Chapter 17
  The Power of Sacrifice 168
Chapter 18
  The Key Of David 180

Chapter One
WHO IS A SNIPER?

Snipe, as defined by the Webster Collegiate Dictionary implies, means to shoot at an exposed individual, (as of an enemy's forces) from a usually concealed point of vantage. A Sniper therefore is one who snipes. Snipers are servicemen belonging to various arms of the military. They are sharpshooters or marksmen from the various services who are trained to be Snipers. Being a Sniper carries a lot more responsibility than being a marksman. A Sniper must make quality decisions on his own. He must be an expert in the art of camouflage and concealment, stalking and stealth. He is involved in reconnaissance; thus, he must be able to relay vital information to the Command Center for artillery fire, bombardment, etc. As a marksman, he can take out desirable targets from a great distance. His targets of interest include: Commanders, Pilots and communication equipment like radars, radios and transmitters. They also target fuel tanks and whatever else will help to disable or slow down the enemy. They are masters at causing confusion in the enemy's camp. Snipers have carved out essential roles in the battlefields of the world. How much more we need spiritual Snipers as we face Satan, his hosts and agents.

The kingdom of God suffers violence; it is assailed by enemy forces. Many gallant infantrymen have been killed. The biblical phrase "kill the shepherd and the flocks will scatter" is still true today. There is a Chinese proverb equivalent which says, "Kill one man, terrorize a thousand." The Sniper wants to disrupt the chain of command and therefore seeks to eliminate enemy

Commanders. A Sniper in this spiritual context is a person whose spirit man is alive and backed by grace (the resources of heaven) and is anointed to pull down principalities and powers, rulers of darkness and wicked spirits in the heavenlies. He is anointed to eliminate satanic agents in their different facets (religious, governmental or individuals) through the efficacy of prayers that cannot fail.

Below are some of the characteristics of a Sniper:

1   He knows who to pray to (The Father).
2   He knows what to ask (in accordance with the word).
3   He does not ramble, use many words, vain words or spray bullets like a machine gun.
4   He knows what the will of God is.
5   He is sincere in prayer.
6   He does not have ulterior motives.
7   He is concise, uses his cross hairs.
8   He does not pretend.
9   He takes things point by point.
10   He does not jumble prayers together.
11   He arranges and prepares his petition.
12   He is incredibly detailed and specific.
13   He believes "one bullet, one result."
14   He has eagle-eye vision.
15   His eyes are single.
16   He knows when to stop.
17   He knows when to rest awhile (Sabbath).
18   He knows when to resume his watch.
19   He knows nothing is impossible with God.
20   He knows nothing is impossible to him as a believer.
21   He is earnest in prayer.
22   He knows what supplication is.
23   He knows how to intercede.
24   He knows how to give thanks.

25   He knows angels are on assignment on his behalf.
26   He knows God's armory.
27   He chooses his weapon of choice an M403A (spirit man)
28   He knows about the weapon of fire like Elijah.
29   He can call in the plagues like Moses.
30   He can split an altar in twain like the young prophet from Judah.
31   He can send a bolt of lightning (word) on an errand.
32   He is a master at his trade.
33   He puts his faith into action.
34   He knows where to lay ambush for his enemy.
35   He waits patiently to get his prize.
36   He blesses the Lord at all times.
37   He praises the Lord always.
38   He calls sin "sin" and not by some fancy name (alternative lifestyle).
39   He knows he is a target of the enemy also.
40   He does not give place to the devil.
41   He has killed the sin of:

- *Pride*
- *Gluttony*
- *Selfishness*
- *Adultery*
- *Fornication*
- *Masturbation, etc.*

42   He takes calculated risks.
43   He eats what is needed.
44   He cannot take a bathroom break while on his watch.
45   He does not lap water like a dog.
46   He is righteous.
47   He is bold as a lion.
48   He is motivated by his love for the (nation) kingdom of God.
49   He has great faith.
50   He is faithful.

51   He has the keys of David.
52   He rejoices in the Lord.
53   He is glad.
54   He is joyful.
55   He is a watchman.
56   He watches over his household.
57   He watches over the household of God.
58   He watches his city.
59   He watches over his state.
60   He does service to his nation.
61   He reads the bible.
62   He meditates on the Word.
63   He washes his feet with butter.
64   He has been to the Altar of Sacrifice.
65   He has the golden censer in his hands.
66   He has access to the Holiest of All.
67   He does not meddle.
68   He does not entangle himself in the affairs of life.
69   He does not lie.
70   He does not backbite.
71   He is not a gossip.
72   He has the mind of Christ.
73   He is alive in his spirit.
74   His soul is subject to his Spirit.
75   His body is subject to him.
76   He is seated in heavenly places in Christ.
77   He is far above principalities and powers.
78   He is above rulers of darkness and wicked spirits.
79   He sets guard over his heart and mouth.
80   He has surrendered his tongue to the Holy Spirit.
81   He speaks the word only.
82   He does not catch a cold.
83   He does not sneeze, nay not on his watch.
84   He does not fall sick.
85   He has Yehovah-Rapha as his healer.

86   He has entered into divine health.
87   He is strong and alert.
88   He blends with his surroundings.
89   He has learned the art of silence.
90   He knows the thunder of silence.
91   He hears from God.
92   He operates in the gifts of the Holy Spirit.
93   He calls unbelief sin.
94   He has no guile.
95   He loves the Lord with all his heart.
96   He loves the brethren.
97   He is the head and not the tail.
98   He is above only and not beneath.
99   He lends and does not borrow.
100   He is victorious.

Chapter Two
HOLY GHOST INVASION CORPS SNIPER SCHOOL

The Unites States of America has a Sniper training school called the United States Marine Corps Scout Sniper School (USMCSSS). Here, men who have distinguished themselves in the various services are trained to become Snipers. However, not all graduate from this school. A great amount of time is spent in physical training, range practice, use of scopes and measuring distances or rather range of target. They learn about ballistics. Ballistics is the scientific study about projectiles and how they are affected by wind, barometric pressure, temperature and gravity. The Sniper training is broken into three primary areas. They are: Marksmanship, Observation and Stalking.

Marksmanship is the ability to put the bullet where it counts, against all odds. Sometimes, it is a moving target.

Observation – Observation is the ability to grasp and define the finest details of your terrain, for vantage position, for concealment, delivery of the lightning bolt, retreat and also for reporting to the Command Center for reconnaissance purposes.

Stalking: This is a great asset to a Sniper and the reason why many fail to graduate from the Sniper school. It is the ability to sneak as close as possible, day or night, to a given target without being detected

These same objectives and more are the necessary skills and training needed for a spiritual Sniper. A Sniper's prayer rends the heavens. Jesus, the greatest Sniper of all time, rends the heavens in His ministry. At the baptism of John and at the transfiguration,

Jesus rends the heavens.

"*This is my beloved son in whom I am well pleased.*" Matthew 3:17

Stephen, a man of great faith, rends the heavens. God is looking for men who will rend the heavens in our generation. God is looking for men who will say "*in the pages of the book it is written of me; to do thy will, Oh God.*"

At twelve years of age, Jesus knew he had to be about His Father's business. He knew the temple was His dwelling place. No wonder the Psalmist, King David, cried for the courts of our Lord. He spent time in the secret place, on the mountain top and came down to release only the word that brings results.

Prayer is a vital and conscious union with God. It is the place of Holy communion with God. It is the secret place of the Most High. Oh, that all would enroll today in God's Holy Ghost Invasion Snipers School! You would imagine that there are many ministers enrolled in this school. The truth is far from it. You would think it may be 10% or 5%; however, it would be a miracle to find 1% enrollment in this school. I hear the voice of the Lord saying "*Go away with your sacrifices! Go away with your oblations from an unholy priesthood. Because of this evil, I am changing the guards, just like I shut the womb of Hannah until she cried to me and made a covenant with me to offer me a son. I am looking for a Church that will cry unto me and offer unto me her first born whom I will raise up as a replacement and shall be a holy priesthood after the order of Melchizedek.*"

God is moving outside the ministerial fold to lay people who will enroll in this school, so that with them, He might confound the so-called "*ministers.*" How many ministers, like the prophets of Baal, gyrate and shout from morning until evening and no fire falls from heaven?

The temple of God has become a place to sell prayer cloths, silver wares, olive oil and much more. According to Jesus, it has become a den of thieves instead of a house of prayer. 1 Cor 3:16 says that our bodies are the temple of the Holy Spirit. In Hebrews, the word for "temple" is "Beth." The same word "Beth" is the word for house. His house (us, our bodies) is the house of prayer for all nations. This means that every member of the Body of Christ is called to be a house of prayer for all nations.

Who are thou, O Great Mountain, before the Sniper? Thou shall become a plain and he shall bring forth the headstone shouting Grace! Grace!! Selah. EFOV

David of old took one stone (bullet) to fell Goliath. A stone cut without a hand destroyed the image in the book of Daniel. God's Snipers will establish the Kingdom of God on earth. A Sniper knows the heart of God and thus prays the mind of God. Solomon said, "*For thou, O LORD of hosts, God of Israel, hast revealed to thy servant, saying, I will build thee an house: therefore hath thy servant found in his heart to pray this prayer unto thee.* 2 Samuel 7:27

Our Lord Jesus Christ said,

"*I do nothing of my own but what I see my Father do, the same doeth the Son likewise.*" John 5:30.

Men like Nehemiah, Daniel and Jeremiah, found out the mind of God and prayed it back to Him. When the mind of God echoes back to heaven by a surrendered vessel in the earth, it releases power from heaven for God's will to be made manifest.

God's provided way is the only way. In many African traditions, the way to approach a King is to come with Kola nuts and a bottle of whiskey. However, you may choose to come with a brand-new car, a very big cake and a greeting card, which is not protocol. They will still demand that you follow protocol. Abel, we are told, offered a more acceptable sacrifice than Cain. What made the difference? Abel had the revelation of the mind of God. By faith, he knew God's acceptable protocol was blood because he saw the pattern that God had already established in covering the nakedness of Adam by a sacrifice. He could only have done that by faith which comes by hearing and hearing by the word of God, not by presumption. The Sniper has been trained to enter into God's secret place. There he has trained his spirit man and learned the principles of ballistics (the spoken word);

"...so shall my word be that goeth forth out of my mouth: it shall not return unto me void..." Isaiah 55:11.

The Sniper hears and has the ears of God and thus, is in communication with his Command Center.

My son, attend to my words; incline thine ear unto my sayings. Proverbs 4:20, 22:17

It is very essential to study the following scriptures: II Kings 19:16; Nehemiah 1:6,11; Psalms 10:17; Psalms 17:6, Psalms 31:2, Psalms 71:2, Psalms 86:1, Psalms 88:2, Psalms 102:2; Proverbs 5:1; Isaiah 37:17; Lamentation 3:56; Daniel 9:18

Faith and prayers are learned skills. They are learned at God's shooting range daily. You can only learn to pray by praying and faith comes by hearing and marksmanship comes by speaking the word of God. Yesterday's faith and prayers have become stale today and like overnight manna, have bred worms. Practice, practice, practice is the key to becoming a great Sniper. Wavering faith will not hit the bull's eye. Asking amiss is a waste of efforts. The lack of observation will only make a Christian a prey.

"A wise man foresees an evil and hides, but a fool walks into the trap and is destroyed." Proverbs 22:3.

God has given us gifts of the Spirit that see things, that say things and of power that does things. It is time to go back to the elementary stuff in Christianity. We all need to graduate from drinking milk and be thoroughly equipped as a soldier and then come to enroll in the Holy Ghost Invasion Corps Sniper School. It is important to note that a Sniper is sometimes able to hit targets over 1000 yards away but God's Snipers can pray in Africa or America and hit a target anywhere in the world or beyond, just as Joshua who stopped the sun and the moon in their place for about an entire day (Joshua10:12). How amazing!!!

Chapter Three
A SNIPER'S PRAYER

One God, the creator of the
One Rifle (the spirit man) that delivers the
One (Silver) Bullet; Give me
One Chance and let me seize the
One Moment as I am in
One Accord with you to bring in the
One Result in the Name of the
One Jesus who is the
One, Amen.

The Sniper's prayer is his code of belief and conduct.

ONE GOD

The Sniper believes in one God who is the Absolute and the only Potentate. The Igbo call Him Chukwu Okike - One God. The Yoruba call him, Olodumare - the King of kings and the Lord of lords. The Esan call Him Osenobula - bigger than all. The Sniper is not confused with the mystery of the Godhead. There is no confusion whatsoever in his mind who to pray to. He relies on the biblical testimony, "Hear O Israel the Lord thy God is One Lord." He believes that God is sovereign and does whatever He wills in the army of heaven and none can ask Him, "What doest thou?" The Sniper knows what omnipotence means and does not ascribe power to Satan, demons, kings, man, elements, the atom, hydrogen bombs or so called "super powers." God is the power that be. As an adopted son of God, he shares in God's omnipotence. His God is Omniscient - all knowing and he enjoys that privilege through a word of wisdom, a word of knowledge and discerning of spirits. The omnipresence of God is his blessed assurance that he is not alone and that angels, ministering spirits are at his beck and call. Jesus Christ said He could make requisition to headquarters and twelve legions of angels would be at His disposal. Using the Roman legion of six thousand men, that would be seventy - two thousand angels. Through the fire and through the water, the Sniper is confident because he is engraven in the palm of the Lord; he is the apple of God's eye.

ONE RIFLE

"The LORD hath opened his armory, and hath brought forth the weapons of his indignation: for this is the work of the Lord GOD of hosts in the land..." Jeremiah 50:25

The Sniper goes to his armory and selects a rifle. The M40A3 is his favorite rifle. He knows how to dismantle his rifle and skillfully put it together again. He knows the power of the anointing oil. He oils all the necessary parts. He checks the barrel. A barrel is a conduit; it must not have any flaws. It must be straight. He must walk a straight path. Whatever he has to deliver must have a free flow or passage. Nothing must color it up or be added to what must be delivered. So, he walks the path of holiness without which no man can see God. He checks his trigger, making sure it slides properly and smoothly. The Sniper is very versatile and, as in a Chemistry laboratory, he knows how to trigger crystallization. He is familiar with how an avalanche can be triggered. He knows what it takes to trigger the coming revival. He knows that the map of Africa is shaped like a revolver and that Nigeria is the trigger. So, he works his trigger carefully because he knows the trigger is tied to the Kairos, (opportune moment) in that split second. As a surveyor, he is well accustomed to cross-hairs, so he checks his line of sight as he looks through the telescopic sight and makes the necessary adjustments. It must hit the bull's eye with perfect precision. He knows the way of the eagle and perfect vision is non- negotiable.

"For the eyes of the LORD run to and fro throughout the whole earth, to shew himself strong in the behalf of them whose heart is perfect toward him." 2 Chronicles 16:9.

Darkness is noon day to him because of his night vision equipment. Next, he checks the hammer. It has been adequately anointed to send the word (silver bullet).

Is not my word like as a fire? saith the LORD; and like a hammer that breaketh the rock in pieces? Jeremiah 23:29

Cast forth lightning, and scatter them: shoot out thine arrows, and destroy them. Psalms 144:6

As teenagers, we used to play on the word Warsaw saying *"Warsaw never saw war until war saw Warsaw."* My dear friends, you cannot sit on the fence; war is coming to you.

"Thou art my battle axe and weapons of war: for with thee will I break in pieces the nations, and with thee will I destroy kingdoms; And with thee will I break in pieces the horse and his rider; and with thee will I break in pieces the chariot and his rider; With thee also will I break in pieces man and woman; and with thee will I break in pieces old and young; and with thee will I break in pieces the young man and the maid;
I will also break in pieces with thee the shepherd and his flock; and

with thee will I break in pieces the husbandman and his yoke of oxen; and with thee will I break in pieces captains and rulers." Jeremiah 51:20-23

God declares of the Sniper *"Thou art my battle axe and weapons of war."* The spirit of man, the real you or the hidden man of the heart is what God is talking about. One thing that has not ceased to amaze me is about someone who is *"born again into witchcraft"* or initiated into witchcraft. It does not matter how young or old; he or she enters the *"spiritual realm,"* and they begin to increase in wickedness. However, Christians that are born again know nothing of the supernatural realm and walk as mere men with;

"… bitter envying and strife in your hearts…" James 3:14.

"…sensual, having not the Spirit." Jude 1:19

Their spirit man was born again but they slipped back into the natural. They were not instructed on how to develop the inward man. The scripture;

"… man shall not live by bread alone, but by every word of God" (Luke 4:4);

should be a great reminder of what we have failed to do. Joshua was explicitly told how to prosper and have good success in life through meditating in the word. We have fed the beastly part of us and we have starved the Lamb to death. Paul who excelled spiritually said, "

For I delight in the law of God after the inward man." Romans 7:22.

He developed his inward man. He further said,

"For which cause we faint not; but though our outward man perish, yet the inward man is renewed day by day." 2 Corinthians 4:16

"But let it be the hidden man of the heart, in that which is not corruptible, even the ornament of a meek and quiet spirit, which is in the sight of God of great price." 1 Peter 3:4

True service and worship are in the spirit. All else is vain.

"For God is my witness, whom I serve with my spirit in the gospel of his Son, that without ceasing I make mention of you always in my prayers" Romans 1:9

"But he is a Jew, which is one inwardly; and circumcision is that of the heart, in the spirit, and not in the letter; whose praise is not of men, but of God." Romans 2:29

The word of God is what does the intricate operation of separating our spirit from the death grip of the soul. The word of God not only separates but maintains and nurtures the spirit, giving him governing authority. Many today use the scripture;

"...the spirit indeed is willing, but the flesh is weak" (Matt 26:41);

as an escape or to excuse their failures.

The book of Romans 6-7, should be thoroughly digested by believers so we can rightly credit our account,

"…that we should serve in newness of spirit, and not in the oldness of the letter." Romans 7:6

"There is therefore now no condemnation to them which are in Christ Jesus, who walk not after the flesh, but after the Spirit." Romans 8:1

The Scriptures are clear about the futility of the flesh in spiritual matters when the Apostle Paul declared:

"But the natural man receiveth not the things of the Spirit of God: for they are foolishness unto him: neither can he know them, because they are spiritually discerned." 1 Corinthians 2:14.

"For what man knoweth the things of a man, save the spirit of man which is in him? Even so the things of God knoweth no man, but the Spirit of God." 1 Corinthians 2:11

"Having therefore these promises, dearly beloved, let us cleanse ourselves from all filthiness of the flesh and spirit, perfecting holiness in the fear of God." 2 Corinthians 7:1

The heart and spirit are used interchangeably in scriptures. Man is made up of Spirit, Soul and Body. Great *"spiritual"* capacity can be attained by the power of the soul - Psychics, Mediums, Unity Science, New Age and Buddhist, etc. Watchman Nee in his book, *The Latent Power of The Soul* addresses this issue. The real order is this. The Spirit is the mistress of the house, the soul is the steward and does a lot of carry-on and the body is the slave. When the bible talks about the flesh, it is really talking about the senses.

"And I, brethren, could not speak unto you as unto spiritual, but as unto carnal, even as unto babes in Christ." 1 Corinthians 3:1.

We have lived too long in the nursery. It is time to grow up into maturity and take our place as sons; thus the Sniper is spiritual and not carnal and can be a true delivery system with all integral parts working in sync.

ONE BULLET

The Sniper uses one bullet only. He is extremely confident in his expertise. His motto is "one man, one bullet." He does not need to reload and try again. It is a silver bullet. Silver stands for redemption. It is the price for redemption; however, this also has a tip of brass. Brass means judgment which signifies that the prince of this world is judged.

"And I, if I be lifted up from the earth, will draw all men unto me."
John 12:32

There are different calibers of bullets for different targets. He chooses the appropriate caliber because he must mortally wound his enemy. Ahab went into battle in disguise and along with him went Jehoshaphat fully clad in his kingly regalia.

The Sniper knows that the word is God's messenger and must accomplish that where unto it has been sent. It will not fall to the ground. It shall not come back void. Heaven and earth shall pass away but God's word (silver bullet) shall not fail. The word that heals the sick and brings deliverance is the same that knocks away sickness, diseases, demons and Satan.

The silver bullet released by the Prophet Elijah found its way through the armor of Ahab, mortally wounding him.

"And a certain man drew a bow at a venture, and smote the king of Israel between the joints of the harness: wherefore he said unto the driver of his chariot, Turn thine hand, and carry me out of the host; for I am wounded." I Kings 22:34

"So shall my word be that goeth forth out of my mouth: it shall not return unto me void, but it shall accomplish that which I please, and

it shall prosper in the thing whereto I sent it." Isaiah 55:11

"With God, nothing shall be impossible" and nothing shall be impossible to the Sniper who believes." Luke 1:37 EFOV

The word of God shall not be void of power. It will and must hit its target. It must accomplish or perform according to the pronouncement. Jesus sent His word and His word healed them. The word of God is infallible and does not need help from man. The word creates and upholds all things. One word from God is all it takes. The spoken word is the original seed (stem cell). This last great revival shall be characterized by the spoken word *"According to my word so shall it be."* See my book, *There shall Be A Performance.*

"Thou sawest till that a stone was cut out without hands, which smote the image upon his feet that were of iron and clay, and brake them to pieces. Then was the iron, the clay, the brass, the silver, and the gold, broken to pieces together, and became like the chaff of the summer threshing floors; and the wind carried them away, that no place was found for them: and the stone that smote the image became a great mountain, and filled the whole earth." Daniel 2:34-35

A stone was all it took to take away the reproach of Israel from Goliath and the Philistine army (1 Samuel 17:49). It will only take one stone to take away the reproach of the Christ that the Kingdom of God might be established. The enemy must be mortally wounded. You cannot let him live to fight another day. God's silver bullet, from an anointed and holy vessel, cannot fall short. It is like a thunderbolt; a flash of lightning and the enemy is no more.

"For the word of God is quick, and powerful, and sharper than any two-edged sword, piercing even to the dividing asunder of soul and spirit, and of the joints and marrow, and is a discerner of the

thoughts and intents of the heart." Hebrews 4:12

I pray today you will begin to speak (smite) with the word (stone, bullet) the Goliath (strongman) that has brought reproach to your life. May you assign a bullet to every image and idol and may they be brought down by a lightning bolt. In Jesus' name!

ONE CHANCE

"I returned, and saw under the sun, that the race is not to the swift, nor the battle to the strong, neither yet bread to the wise, nor yet riches to men of understanding, nor yet favor to men of skill; but time and chance happeneth to them all." Ecclesiastes 9:11

The Philistines took the ark of God into the temple of their god, Dagon. Dagon was punished and so were the people with emerods, (Hemorrhoids). They wanted to know if their affliction was a matter of chance (1 Samuel 6:9). The chance we are talking about has no probability of failure. You are not a helpless pawn left to circumstances or gambling but you create and call it forth by the power of omnipotence. Joshua told the sun and the moon to stand still and they obeyed him. He created the atmosphere to accomplish his task. The Sniper is very well acquainted with these scriptures:

"...And it is turned round about by his counsels: that they may do whatsoever he commandeth them upon the face of the world in the earth." Job 37:12

Yehovah, the all-powerful, creates the opportunities so He does not need a second chance. The Sniper walks with God. Just like Moses, the Sniper understands God's ways but the children of Israel knew only His acts. He can call frogs, fleas, fires, hailstones, etc. The creative word is in His mouth.

Many decades ago, I had just finished a prayer meeting at Akoka in Lagos, Nigeria. I walked about half a mile to the major freeway to get a bus. It was late, nearing midnight. Few cars drove by and I waved but none would stop. I thought within myself, I have been away from Lagos so long, no one would know me. I heard the voice of the Lord say, "I know you." Immediately, I called forth a vehicle to take me home in the mighty name of Jesus. It was only a moment later that a bus stopped in front of me. They recognized me. They were Christians coming from a prayer meeting and they lived right across from my father's house - glory hallelujah!

ONE MOMENT

Different Hebrew and Greek words are used for the word "moment."

They imply the blink of an eye, an instant, as when Anna and Simeon came into the temple at the dedication of Jesus Christ. Atomos is an interesting Greek word. It is from "atomos" that the word, atom, derives. It means indivisible, as in split second suddenly. Another interesting Greek word is "Kairos" which implies a set time - in the fullness of time.

The Sniper seizes the moment. There is no time to blink an eye. He takes his aim and pulls the trigger.

"A man hath joy by the answer of his mouth: and a word (bullet) spoken (released) in due season, how good is it!" Proverbs 15:23

Friends, there is a due season for increase and fruitfulness. **Leviticus 26:4**
There is a time of refreshing. **Acts 3:19-21**
There is meat or provision in the due season. **Psalms 104:27; Deuteronomy 11:14**
There is sacrifice in due season. **Numbers 28:2** and Elijah maximized the moment and fire came down from heaven in the

sight of them all.

There is a due season to reap if we faint not. **Galatians 6:9**

For those who are looking for the fruit of the womb, this is your set time!

The Sniper knows God's appointed times and seasons. There is a due season for everything under the sun. He seizes the moment. The long-awaited Messiah was brought into the temple for dedication. Simeon seized and maximized the moment. Anna also did likewise.

"…And he came by the Spirit into the temple…" Read Luke 2:25-32

"…And she, coming in that instant…" Read Luke 2:36-38

What an amazing God and how wonderful it is to be called to this holy calling. Where was the Aaronic Priesthood? Very simple, old folks, well advanced in age (Baby boomers), but they were Snipers. By the Spirit of God, the chance or rather the opportunity came and they seized the moment.

"As many as are led by the Spirit of God they are the mature sons of God." Romans 8:14

God's heart and design this hour is to bypass the unholy priesthood and use the no-names, the nobodies that He might confound the wise. Many ministers will miss out in this next move of God. God is calling out for the Eagle generation that will gather unto Him. They are in preparation and will seize the moment. The fullness of the time is upon us (Galatians 4:4).

At Lystra, Paul perceived in the spirit that the impotent man had faith to be healed. He told the man to stand up (pulled the trigger) and in that instant, the man was healed. The impotent man did three things: He heard Paul preach the Word; he had faith to be healed, he obeyed or responded to the spoken word by standing up and was healed.

Today is your day to be healed. This is the appointed time and to you, I say, "Rise up and be healed in the mighty name of Jesus, Amen!" It is time to dance, shout and praise the LORD!!!

I was told to pray for a lady who had suffered eight miscarriages and two stillbirths. Her moment came two years later. When I perceived in my spirit the place and time of her miracle, I pulled the trigger and the rest is history. She had the miracle of a baby boy to the glory of God.

ONE ACCORD

It is easier for one man to be in accord with himself. As the number of people in an agreement increases, things become more difficult.

This is the way it is in the natural. Jesus said, *"If two of you shall agree."* Matthew18:19

There is power in agreement, being of one mind and one purpose. *"It shall be done."* The word also declares-- *can two walk together unless they are agreed; One shall chase a thousand but two shall chase ten thousand.* The devil is aware of this law of God and tries to bring disunity among the brethren in the church but especially among husbands and wives which is the greatest unity that can achieve God's purpose. In the case of David, when the appointed time came, God caused all Israel to gather unto him to make him king.

"And they helped David against the band of the rovers: for they were all mighty men of valor, and were captains in the host. All these men of war, that could keep rank, came with a perfect heart to Hebron, to

make David king over all Israel: and all the rest also of Israel were of one heart to make David king." 1 Chronicles 12:21-38

"Again I say unto you, that if two of you shall agree on earth as touching anything that they shall ask, it shall be done for them of my Father which is in heaven.

For where two or three are gathered together in my name, there am I in the midst of them." Matthew 18:19-20

Israel gathered in one accord to be presented to their king as in the case of Saul. They had demanded a king to be like other nations. It did not please YHVH but,

When he had caused the tribe of Benjamin to come near by their families, the family of Matri was taken, and Saul the son of Kish was taken: and when they sought him, he could not be found.
Therefore they inquired of the LORD further, if the man should yet come thither. And the LORD answered, Behold, he hath hid himself among the stuff." 1 Samuel 10:21-22

They did not get sniff dogs to find him out. Samuel the Seer, through inquiry from God, located him. The Sniper has to be able to locate his enemies through the gift of God. A word of knowledge or discerning of spirits is needed.

The disciples of Jesus continued with one accord in prayer (Acts 1:14).
On the day of Pentecost, they were all with one accord in one place, a mighty rushing wind came and they were filled with the Holy Spirit (Acts 2:1-4). The walls of Jericho fell as the children of Israel compassed it about in one accord according to the God given instruction (Joshua 6:2-15).

Gideon's army had an amazing victory as the three companies

blew the trumpets, broke the pitchers, held the lamps in their left hands and the trumpets in their right hand and they cried, the sword of the LORD, and of Gideon. (Judges 7:16-22)

The only accord we seem to have in our churches today is discord. We have racial and ethnic churches and within is in-fighting. It is time to break the walls and to experience a greater glory than they enjoyed at the dedication of Solomon's temple.

"…as the trumpeters and singers were as one, to make one sound to be heard in praising and thanking the LORD…. that then the house was filled with a cloud, even the house of the LORD.. So that the priests could not stand to minister by reason of the cloud: for the glory of the LORD had filled the house of God". 2 Chronicles 5:13-14

The Lord acknowledged the power of oneness in the building of the Tower of Babel and said:

"…and now nothing will be restrained from them, which they have imagined to do…" Genesis 11:6

There is power in being in one accord and Jesus' prayer is that we may be one and one in Him. There is a false accord today in the United Nations also among the World Council of Churches, just as it was in the time of Jesus the Christ; they formed the Sanhedrin Council to oppose the Gospel. True Unity or Accord is in the Word. God will not judge us by your Church affiliation or denomination but only by the Word that lives and abides forever. The big question is, "What is your conformity?"; The world or the Word? Satan knows about this power and fights the basic unity in the home, husband and wife - accord. The Sniper is in one accord with his environment so you cannot search him out. He is in one accord with his equipment by reason of use, mastery and expertise. Above all, he is in one accord with God. He knows the value and power of oneness and like Jesus on the

Cross, he cannot bear separation from His Father. When Jesus said that they may be one-- *I in you and you in me* (the divine sandwich), the Snipers took a hold of that and never would let it go. Like Jesus, they can make declarations like-- *"I say unto you; according to my word,"* because they have become the oracle of God. In the case of Gideon's armies, as they were in one accord to do in accordance with the word, the enemies began to self-destruct. The victory over Jericho was because of being in one accord. Whenever there is a breach, discord or disharmony as in the case of Achan, Israel lost their battle against Ai. Sin is discord. A discordant tone in a great orchestra brings disharmony and the symphony and the beauty is lost.

"If I regard iniquity in my heart, the Lord will not hear me."
Psalms 66:18

Are you the Achan in the midst or the flea in the oil? God wants a Church without spot or wrinkle or anything that defiles. That Church must come forth, which would be overshadowed and impregnated by the Holy Spirit to bring forth the Man-Child, (Snipers, the stature of the perfect man) that would rule with a rod of iron. We are told of Jesus;

"...in Him dwelleth the fullness of the Godhead bodily." Colossians 2:9;

Of this group, hear this amazing testimony,

*"... to know the love of Christ, which passeth knowledge, **that ye might be filled with all the fullness of God.**"* Ephesians 3:14-19

The Sniper is in one accord with his Spirit, Soul and Body. Once again, he is a perfect man and bears the Name of his God. Like Paul, I pray this prayer for you—

And the very God of peace sanctify you wholly; and I pray God your whole spirit and soul and body be preserved blameless unto the coming of our Lord Jesus Christ.
Faithful is he that calleth you, who also will do it."
1 Thessalonians 5:23-24

ONE RESULT

"LORD, thou hast heard the desire of the humble." Psalms 10:17, 21:2, 38:9

"Then said I, Lo, I come: in the volume of the book it is written of me,
I delight to do thy will, O my God: yea, thy law is within my heart." Psalms 40:6-8

"And mine eye hath seen his desire upon mine enemies." Psalms 54:7, 70:2, 59:10 92:11)

"Whom have I in heaven but thee and there is none upon earth that I desire beside thee."

"Satisfiest the desire of every living thing."
Psalms 145:16, 19; Prov 10:24

"The desire of the righteous is only good; it is a tree of life and sweet to the soul and it is to the name of the Lord and the remembrance of Him." Prov 11:23, 13:12,19; Isa 26:8; Ps 73:25

"For verily I say unto you, That whosoever shall say unto this mountain, Be thou removed, and be thou cast into the sea; and shall not doubt in his heart, but shall believe that those things which he saith shall come to pass; he shall have whatsoever he saith. Therefore I say unto you, What things soever ye desire, when ye pray, believe that ye receive them, and ye shall have them." Mark 11:23-24

When Jesus spoke to the fig tree, we saw the desired result. The word declares *"…the desire of the righteous shall not be cut off…"*. The result is certain. There is no room for alternates, if this does not happen then----. Faith never fails and never fails to obtain the desired result.

The one result the Sniper needs is fruitfulness. He has spent a lot of time (Chronos) to reach the kairos (opportuned time). He cannot fail. He cannot miss. In the life of Joseph, with the many dreams came along the forces of hell to frustrate him-- bitterness, pain, imprisonment and abandonment all stared him in the face for so many years but the **One Moment** came to get the **One Result** and failure was not an option. Simon said *"… I have waited for the salvation…"* Joseph stepped up to the plate having washed himself and shaven. Today he now puts on a new Coat which no one can take away from him. The One Result wiped away the barrenness and unfruitfulness of yester years. He stood before Pharaoh and now the dream becomes reality. He is made Prime Minister in Egypt. In the naming of his sons we see the process. His first was Manasseh, which means —- Causing to forget--

"Joseph called the name of the firstborn Manasseh: For God has made me forget all my toil and all my father's house." Genesis 41:51.

He called the second Ephraim, which means-----twice or doubly fruitful.

"And the name of the second, called he Ephraim: For God has caused me to be fruitful in the land of my affliction." Genesis 41:52

He, like Paul, was declaring-- *forgetting the past and moving on to get a hold of that* **One Result**-- *the mark of the high calling in Christ Jesus.* David desired one thing *"to dwell in His presence"* because that will always produce the **One Result**. In the life of

Peter, we see the offering of the boat and the commandment to pull out into the deep. The command to cast the net on the right side brought about a net breaking and boat sinking miraculous catch of fish. He was then told-- from now on he would catch men. Jesus was crucified and they all felt that all hope was lost. Some disciples on the way to Emmaus said *"...it was he..."* Now, Peter stood up during the mourning season and said, *"...I go a fishing..."* They labored and caught nothing until Jesus came on the scene. Jesus said unto them;

"Children, have ye any meat? They answered him, 'No.'
And he said unto them, Cast the net on the right side of the ship, and ye shall find. They cast therefore, and now they were not able to draw it for the multitude of fishes..As soon then as they were come to land, they saw a fire of coals there, and fish laid thereon, and bread.....
Jesus saith unto them, Come and dine." John 21:1-12

I believe this experience was forever ingrained in the life of Peter--- *"...Lovest thou me more than these...?"* The due season of Pentecost came and Peter stood and 3000 souls came into the Kingdom. The next was 5000 saved. The birth pangs bring the **One Result** – The Man-child. Hannah's cry and travail brought forth Samuel. Jesus endured the cross and the shame for the joy that was set before him. Paul declares: "

"...the suffering of this present time is nothing to be compared to the glory which shall be revealed in us." Romans 8:18

Concerning Joseph, we are told:

"Joseph is a fruitful bough, even a fruitful bough by a well; whose branches run over the wall." Genesis 49:22

"And he shall be like a tree planted by the rivers of water, that

bringeth forth his fruit in his season; his leaf also shall not wither; and whatsoever he doeth shall prosper." Psalms 1:3

I would like to end with this one thought "The One Name Jesus guarantees the **One Result**" Amen.

God will frustrate the desire of the wicked against you and their weapons shall not prosper In Jesus Name Amen.

ONE JESUS

This is nothing but the revelation of Jesus Christ. His Name shall be called Jesus for it is He that shall SAVE. Salvation implies healing, deliverance protection, provision etc. In the Name Jesus we have all the redemptive names in the Old Testament. Some believe they have the revelation of the Name, and that is their ticket for the rapture. It is very important to know that *"Jehovah of the Old Testament is the Jesus of the New"* they say. I have seen men who blow hot air, just head knowledge that puffs up. Revelation knowledge is what is needed. In some safe deposits it requires more than one key or codes carried by different people to open the safe. Most of these fellows I know obviously lack the revelation of Yehovah – rapha and are sick in their bodies, they lack the revelation of El-Elyon and the affairs of their lives are nothing to be envied. A true revelation of who Christ is would be to fully appropriate the redemptive Names of God. See my book "The Excellent Name of Jesus."

The Sniper knows who he is "in Him, in Christ, in Whom" etc. He knows he has the power of attorney to use the Name of Jesus. The Name is a strong tower of refuge for him. All things bow to that name and he uses that name because it comes with effect. When he calls that Name, Yehovah shows up. Peter used the name and the lame man at the gate Beautiful, started leaping and praising the Lord.

The apostles baptized in that name and prayed in the wonderful Name of Jesus. The Snipers have the seal and name of God on their foreheads and they manifest His Name. The Sniper knows that he is called by His Name.

ONE AMEN

This word, like Alleluia, is universal and it means truly, faithful, surely, verily, so be it. It is like the judgment given by a judge or a potentate. Pilate said to the Jews, "...*What I have written I have written...*". It was the final verdict on the issue of the inscription on the cross "*Jesus the King of the Jews*" Amen!!

"*Verily, verily, I say unto you, Except a corn of wheat fall into the ground and die, it abideth alone: but if it die, it bringeth forth much fruit.*" John 12:24, 8:34, 16:20

When the word declares "Verily, verily" it is a double verification, a double witness at which every matter shall be established. It is the power of two in agreement on earth and heaven's sanction "*It is done.*" The word "*Amen*" is not a hope or a may be. There is no uncertainty in it. Do not be fooled by the compromise in the Church today and the voice of the Serpent through some preachers declaring "*you shall not surely die*" "*God is a good God*" but forget to say "*God is a Just God*"

"*Verily, verily, I say unto you, Whosoever committeth sin is the servant of sin.*" John 8:34.

".... *against all the houses of the high places which are in the cities of Samaria, shall surely come to pass.*" I Kings 13:32

".... *there shall not be dew nor rain these years, **but according to my word.***" I Kings 17:1

These Prophets spoke with certainty, *"Thus saith the Lord."* This is not a conditional prophecy and there was a performance of every word.

When you say Amen, you are calling on Him who is the Absolute, Elohim who spoke and it was created. You are declaring that the word which you have spoken is out of your hands. His Word is sure, faithful and true. It is God's divine seal and approval on the issue. It is a settled fact. As far as the Sniper is concerned the result is certain and no one can call the bullet back. It cannot fall or fail to hit the bull's eye. His desire and God's desire are fulfilled. Jesus is the Amen.

Chapter Four
The Spirit of Cain

As a little boy, the first assassination I heard of was the assassination of Patrice Lumumba and then, John F. Kennedy. The Sixties seemed to be a time of assassinations as Malcolm X, Martin Luther King JR. and Robert Francis Kennedy, were also killed. Benigno Aquino was assassinated on August 21st 1983; His wife, Corazon Aquino later became the first woman President of the Philippines.

"The Day of the Jackal," a novel written by Frederick Forsyth is about false identities, a rifle and an assassination plot in relation to the French. I would probably guess De Gaul of France who escaped various assassination attempts. The movie definitely portrays the confidence of the man.

Many assassinations have been carried out all over the world. Many of them were politically motivated, some were carried out by fanatics and some have been government sponsored. This is nothing but murder for hire. Various means have been used in the varied assassinations such as guns (Rifles, Short gun, Revolver, etc.), strapping explosives, car bombs and sometimes poison.

Murder is evil and condemned by the Word of God. Cain was the first murderer. The second murderer was also an offspring of Cain. The Bible calls Satan a murderer from the beginning and he is the father of lies.

The penalty for murder is death. However, there are deaths that are accidental and for such, a city of refuge was built that the avenger of blood does not kill such a man.

"But if any man hate his neighbor, and lie in wait for him, and rise up against him, and smite him mortally that he die, and fleeth into one of these cities: Then the elders of his city shall send and fetch him thence, and deliver him into the hand of the avenger of blood, that he may die.

Thine eye shall not pity him, but thou shalt put away the guilt of innocent blood from Israel, that it may go well with thee."
Deuteronomy 19:11-13

Assassinations

Abraham Lincoln was shot on Good Friday of April 14[th,] 1865 a little after 10:00 pm. while watching a play "Our American Cousin" at the **Ford Theater**. He died the next day.

John F Kennedy was shot also on Friday, Nov. 22, 1963, almost 100 years later in Dallas, Texas riding in a **Ford car**.

Other Assassinations of US Presidents:

James A. Garfield – Sat. July 2nd, 1881.
William McKinley – Friday Sept. 6, 1901.

Assassinations Around the World
Patrice Lumumba - 17th January 1961.
Malcolm X – Sunday Feb. 21, 1965. The followers of Elijah Mohammed/ Nation of Islam are thought to be behind this assassination.
Chief Albert Luthuli- July 21, 1967.
Martin Luther King, Jr. – Thursday April 4, 1968.
Robert F. Kennedy, – Wednesday June 5, 1968.
Eduardo Mondlane- On 3 February 1969.
Amilcar Cabral- January 20, 1973.
General Muritala Muhammed of Nigeria – Friday the 13th of

February 1976.

Anwar Sadat. On October 6, 1981.

Israeli Prime Minister Yitzhak Rabin was assassinated November 4, 1995

The assassination of Nigeria's Minister of Justice /Attorney General, Bola Ige was on December 23, 2001

Mr. Anthony Olufunsho Williams (a Governorship aspirant in Lagos State, Nigeria) on Wednesday, 27th July 2006.

Dr. Ayodele Daramola (a Governorship aspirant in Ekiti State, Nigeria) on 14th August 2006.

General Sani Abacha of Nigeria carried out systematic assassinations of people who opposed his regime and could be considered the father of this evil that now plagues Nigeria.

Many faceless and shameless governments in Africa have been involved in assassinations of political opponents.

General Augusto Pinochet of Chile was behind many assassinations of Chileans both at home and abroad.

Assassination attempts

Gamal Abd al-Nasser - October 26, 1954

Kwame Nkrumah. Attempts made in 1962 and 1964

Ronald Reagan's was on March 30, 1981

Prayer

O earth, earth, earth that have drunk of the blood of the slain, rise up against the perpetrators of these evils. Let the avenger of blood pursue the wicked until they are destroyed from the face of the earth. As Cain was marked, let them be marked for destruction.

Today, many Christians backbite and devour one another. The Spirit of Cain is in the Churches. The Sermon on the Mount is regarded as obsolete. There is a new prayer movement that wants to annihilate everyone else. I really wonder if they were killed before they became a Christian where they would be today. *"Whosoever does not love his brother is a murderer."* Love is the mark of true discipleship. Anyone who loves not is a murderer. Every murderer has his portion in the Lake that burns with fire and sulfur.

Chapter Five
It Takes a Sniper

In war, Snipers have very important roles to take down specific targets. They are watching out for Commanders, Officers or to destroy supply lines. In the Nigerian civil war, one of the greatest casualties inflicted upon the Nigerian Army by the Rebels was as a result of the work of a Sniper. There was a long supply line convoy including petrol tankers. He shot at the leading fuel tanker and that sent ripple effects causing grave damage and casualties.

It takes a Sniper to kill a Sniper. As a result of this the Army trains what I would call Sniper hunters or Sniper watchers. They scan their territory and try to root out possible Sniper hideouts and take out Snipers. This is where the skill of observation becomes very vital.

Today, there is no doubt in my mind that the devil has his Snipers too. So, we are faced with not only the call to be Snipers but to also be Sniper hunters. The word of knowledge is indispensable in order to achieve this goal. Let us look at the story of Elisha and the King of Syria.

"Then the king of Syria warred against Israel, and took counsel with his servants, saying, In such and such a place shall be my camp.

And the man of God sent unto the king of Israel, saying, Beware that thou pass not such a place; for thither the Syrians are come down.

And the king of Israel sent to the place which the man of God told him and warned him of, and saved himself there, not once nor twice.

Therefore the heart of the king of Syria was sore troubled for this thing; and he called his servants, and said unto them, **Will ye not shew me which of us is for the king of Israel?**

And one of his servants said, None, my lord, O king: but Elisha, the prophet that is in Israel, telleth the king of Israel the words that thou speakest in thy bedchamber.

And he said, Go and spy where he is, that I may send and fetch him. And it was told him, saying, Behold, he is in Dothan.

Therefore sent he thither horses, and chariots, and a great host: and they came by night, and compassed the city about.

And when the servant of the man of God was risen early, and gone forth, behold, an host compassed the city both with horses and chariots. And his servant said unto him, Alas, my master! how shall we do?

And he answered, Fear not: for they that be with us are more than they that be with them.

And Elisha prayed, and said, LORD, I pray thee, open his eyes, that he may see. And the LORD opened the eyes of the young man; and he saw: and, behold, the mountain was full of horses and chariots of fire round about Elisha.

And when they came down to him, Elisha prayed unto the LORD, and said, Smite this people, I pray thee, with blindness. And he smote them with blindness according to the word of Elisha.

And Elisha said unto them, This is not the way, neither is this the city: follow me, and I will bring you to the man whom ye seek. But he led them to Samaria.

And it came to pass, when they were come into Samaria, that Elisha said, LORD, open the eyes of these men, that they may see. And the LORD opened their eyes, and they saw; and, behold, they were in the midst of Samaria.

And the king of Israel said unto Elisha, when he saw them, My father, shall I smite them? shall I smite them?

And he answered, Thou shalt not smite them: wouldest thou smite those whom thou hast taken captive with thy sword and with thy bow? Set bread and water before them, that they may eat and drink, and go to their master.

And he prepared great provision for them: and when they had eaten and drunk, he sent them away, and they went to their master. So the bands of Syria came no more into the land of Israel." II Kings 6:8-33.

Elisha is a typical example of a Sniper hunter.   Joseph and Daniel in the Old Testament had the interpretation of dreams and understood dark sentences. There were lots of Seers in that era.   Today, we have the Holy Spirit and the gifts of the Spirit. We need to develop the gifts of the Holy Spirit as we get into spiritual warfare. This is the era of the Holy Spirit. Let us awaken to His Operation, Manifestation and Administration in our age.

The Sniper needs reasonable time to get acclimatized to the terrain and know if there are changes. He needs time to dig in and be very effective in his work. My opinion is that before any major combat like the Iraq war or the attack on Fallujah and Ramadi, Snipers ought to be in place. Movement of big units will cause the enemy to disperse or dig in. I am not here to discuss the rightness or wrongness of the war but to look at natural perspectives and relate them to the spiritual that we might wage good warfare.

Absalom overthrew his father David as king and made himself king in Hebron.

"And Absalom sent for Ahithophel the Gilonite, David's counselor, from his city, even from Giloh, while he offered sacrifices. And the conspiracy was strong; for the people increased continually with Absalom."
2 Samuel 15:12

Now Ahithophel, a wise man, an anointed Sniper with great counsel, joined ranks with the rebels. His counsel was like the voice of God. When David had knowledge of this, he knew that spelt big trouble for him. He had to pray a Sniper's prayer

"*O LORD, I pray thee, turn the counsel of Ahithophel into foolishness.*" 2 Samuel 15:31

"And it came to pass, that when David was come to the top of the mount, where he worshipped God, behold, Hushai the Archite came to meet him with his coat rent, and earth upon his head:
Unto whom David said, If thou passest on with me, then thou shalt be a burden unto me: But if thou return to the city, and say unto Absalom, I will be thy servant, O king; as I have been thy father's servant hitherto, so will I now also be thy servant: then mayest thou for me defeat the counsel of Ahithophel." 2 Samuel 15:32-34

This was a word of wisdom from David. It takes a thief to catch a thief, so it takes a Sniper to hunt a Sniper.

".....And the counsel of Ahithophel, which he counseled in those days, was as if a man had inquired at the oracle of God: so was all the counsel of Ahithophel both with David and with Absalom."
2 Samuel 16:16-23

"....And Absalom and all the men of Israel said, The counsel of Hushai the Archite is better than the counsel of Ahithophel. For the LORD had appointed to defeat the good counsel of Ahithophel, to the intent that the LORD might bring evil upon Absalom." 2 Samuel 17:1-10

And when Ahithophel saw that his counsel was not followed, he saddled his ass, and arose, and gat him home to his house, to his city, and put his household in order, and hanged himself, and died, and was buried in the sepulcher of his father. 2 Samuel 17:23

Thus was Ahithophel snipped and Absalom and his armies were defeated and the young coup plotter was killed.
Are you a Sniper hunter? Why not enroll today in the School

of the Holy Ghost and Prayer. Robin Hood and William Tell were great archers from movies of yesteryears. They had the skill to pluck an apple from someone's head. We need great Snipers today that can pray or just speak the word only and it shall be so.

David came back to Ziklag and found it had been burnt down and the two wives were taken along with the wives and children of his company. He called Abiathar the priest to bring the ephod. The ephod contains twelves stones and is called the Urim and Thummim. A flash of light would indicate God's pleasure. He prayed specific to the point prayer. Shall I go? Shall I overtake? And the response was *"go, overtake and recover."* For that reason, he set out and got results.

Elijah had a confrontation with Ahab and declared a Sniper's prayer.

"And Elijah the Tishbite, who was of the inhabitants of Gilead, said unto Ahab, As the LORD God of Israel liveth, before whom I stand, there shall not be dew nor rain these years, but according to my word."
I Kings 17:1

"And it came to pass after many days, that the word of the LORD came to Elijah in the third year, saying, Go, shew thyself unto Ahab; and I will send rain upon the earth." I Kings 18:1

Elijah showed himself to Ahab and there were gathered also the 450 priests of Baal and 400 that ministered to Jezebel. Elijah mocked the priests and their god. Their god would not answer and finally Elijah repaired the altar of God which was in ruins. He arranged his sacrifice and asked the workmen to soak it with water and at the time of the evening sacrifice, he called fire from heaven. The Lord heard the prayer of the Sniper. Fire came down from heaven and consumed the sacrifice. Elijah then got hold of the priests of Baal and killed every one of them. It was now time to call forth the rain.

"Behold, there ariseth a little cloud out of the sea, like a man's hand. And he said, Go up, say unto Ahab, Prepare thy chariot, and get thee down, that the rain stop thee not. And it came to pass in the meanwhile, that the heaven was black with clouds and wind, and there was a great rain. And Ahab rode, and went to Jezreel. And the hand of the LORD was on Elijah; and he girded up his loins, and ran before Ahab to the entrance of Jezreel." I Kings 18:43-46

In the book of James, we are told Elijah was a man of like passion as we are. That implies he ate and went to the bathroom like us and yet he prayed and the heavens were shut and there was no rain for 31/2 years and he prayed again and it rained. He knew how to pray a result-oriented prayer, The Sniper's Prayer.

I have no doubt whatsoever in my mind that God is recruiting Snipers, men that would call down fire, men whose word shall not fall to the ground. See my book, *"There Shall Be A Performance."* The creative anointing shall be upon them and they truly shall be called elohim according to Psalm 82.

"God standeth in the congregation of the mighty; he judgeth among the gods." Psalms 82:1

"I have said, Ye are gods; and all of you are children of the Most High." Psalms 82:6

The Antichrist, False Prophets and evil leaders will meet more than their match when the Snipers (sons of God) are made manifest. A prophet like in the Bible days, is on the scene waiting to be manifested in due time and the prophetic generation are in preparation to receive him. The Sniper's bullets are his words. The delivery system or barrel is the mouth and the tongue is the trigger. Faith is the hammer and the heart is the rifle.

Angels are on assignment to bring to pass the Sniper's prayers. For those whose commands or demands are not understood, they would cause the angels to fold their arms. One moment you believe and make your confessions the next you retract or annul your prayers. Not so with the Sniper. He has spent time with the word and by reason of use has become one with the word. He speaks the word only and has no time for frivolities.

Chapter Six
The Trigger

The tongue is the trigger and once words have been spoken, they cannot be withdrawn. The scriptures have a lot to tell us about this little member.

"Be not rash with thy mouth, and let not thine heart be hasty to utter any thing before God: for God is in heaven, and thou upon earth: therefore let thy words be few." Ecclesiastes 5:2

"Suffer not thy mouth to cause thy flesh to sin; neither say thou before the angel, that it was an error: wherefore should God be angry at thy voice, and destroy the work of thine hands?" Ecclesiastes 5:6

The books of Psalms and Proverbs have a lot to tell us about the tongue. Who else can we learn from but from the "Masters" David and Solomon who by reason of use can rightly dissect the subject?

"A fool's lips enter into contention, and his mouth calleth for strokes. A fool's mouth is his destruction, and his lips are the snare of his soul." Proverbs 18:6

"In the multitude of words there wanteth not sin: but he that refraineth his lips is wise." Proverbs 10:19

"He that hath knowledge spareth his words: and a man of understanding is of an excellent spirit. Even a fool, when he holdeth

his peace, is counted wise: and he that shutteth his lips is esteemed a man of understanding." Proverbs 17:27-28

"If any man among you seem to be religious, and bridleth not his tongue, but deceiveth his own heart, this man's religion is vain."
James 1:26

"For in many things we offend all. If any man offend not in word, the same is a perfect man, and able also to bridle the whole body."
James 3:2

"Set a watch, O LORD, before my mouth; keep the door of my lips."
Psalms 141:3

"I said, I will take heed to my ways, that I sin not with my tongue: I will keep my mouth with a bridle, while the wicked is before me."
Psalms 39:1

"He that backbiteth not with his tongue, nor doeth evil to his neighbour, nor taketh up a reproach against his neighbour." Psalms 15:3

The Sniper is not a babbler he knows the specific time to pull on the trigger.

Customs Checkpoint

"Set a watch, O LORD, before my mouth; keep the door of my lips."
Psalms 141:3

Here, the Psalmist is saying to set a guard over my mouth and also the heart from where it proceeds. Let me put it in my own words:

"Lord set a Customs Checkpoint over my heart and over my mouth." The scripture says, "for out of the abundance of the heart the mouth speaketh." Matthew 12:34 EFOV

"For from within, out of the heart of men, proceed evil thoughts, adulteries, fornications, murders, thefts, covetousness, wickedness, deceit, lasciviousness, an evil eye, blasphemy, pride, foolishness:

All these evil things come from within, and defile the man."
Mark 7:21-23

As you enter a Country at its International Airport or at a border crossing, there is a Customs Checkpoint. The government of the land has earmarked some goods or commodities as contraband. Some are very obvious, like cocaine etc., but some are not quite obvious to some travelers. One time I brought brooms made from Palm fronds into the U.S and they seized them, but they let me go with my Egusi and other African food stuff. They are well trained and even told me the names of the African foods. Your familiarity with the Scriptures will let you know what contraband is and thus you will not suffer loss.

What do they do with the contraband goods? You might have seen on the television when the government burnt cocaine worth millions of dollars in a bonfire. Fire is a good antidote as you set guard over your heart.

The blood of Jesus is a very precious weapon. It purges the conscience from dead works to serve the living God. The word of God is a double-edged sword that performs intricate operations, separating the soul and spirit. The problem of man is from an un-regenerated mind. Renewing the mind is a must on a daily basis to displace or dislodge the evil seed trying to take residence. The spoken word *"It is written; get thee behind me Satan still works today."* If only Adam or Eve could have said those words!! Jesus would never have needed to come. Guarding your heart is like keeping your rifle well oiled, prepared and anointed for the day of battle. Jesus Christ said, *"the prince of this world cometh and has nothing in me."* Your faith is the Hammer which once Triggered by the tongue releases the bullet (the word) through the Barrel (the mouth) and it shall not return unto you void but shall accomplish that purpose for which it has been sent. It hits the bull's eye, the target, and it is time to celebrate the victory.

"...This is the victory that overcomes the world, even our Faith."
1 John 5:4

Let us talk more about the tongue. The tongue can no man tame we are told. Various animals, serpents and beasts have been tamed by man. This trigger-happy tongue has done more evil than all the members combined. There are trigger happy cops who have cost many their lives. They hide under the badge but God's bullet (word) will find them out. That is the reason afflictions come to many Cop families. Unrighteous Judges who have stained their hands with the blood of the innocent are under such condemnation as the "Avenger of blood" seeks them out.

What can we do to the tongue? Or how can we tame the tongue? Since no man can, let us offer it to the Holy Ghost and fire.

The Righteous and his tongue

- *"And my tongue shall speak of thy righteousness and of thy praise all the day long."* Psalms 35:2
- *"The mouth of the righteous speaketh wisdom, and his tongue talketh of judgment."* Psalms 37:30

- *"The mouth of the just bringeth forth wisdom."* Proverbs 10:31

- *"The lips of the righteous know what is acceptable."* Proverbs 10:32

- *"The tongue of the just is as choice silver."* Proverbs 10:20

- *"….the tongue of the wise is health."* Proverbs 12:18

- *"A wholesome tongue is a tree of life."* Proverbs 15:4

The wicked have not set the Lord over them.

"Who have said, With our tongue will we prevail; our lips are our own: who is lord over us?"
Psalms 12:4

Evil tongue

- *"Thy tongue deviseth mischiefs; like a sharp razor, working deceitfully."* Psalms 52:2

- *……deceitful tongue.* Psalms 52:4

- *……tongue a sharp sword.* Psalms 57:4

- *……but the mouth of the wicked speaketh frowardness.* Proverbs 10:32

- *……lying lips, deceitful tongue.* Psalms 120:2

- *……thou false tongue?* Psalms 120:3

- *….a naughty tongue.* Proverbs 17:4

- *….a froward heart a perverse tongue falleth into mischief.*

Proverbs 17:20

- *"….mouth of fools poureth out foolishness.* Proverbs 15:2

- *…..flattering lips, and the tongue that speaketh proud things.* Psalms 12:3

Chapter Seven
A MAN OF VIOLENCE

People consider the Sniper a man of violence. Of a truth he is but his violence is not directed at individuals to hurt, kill or maim. That is the work of the devil and his agents (assassins) who come to steal, kill and destroy. The Sniper on the other hand realizes that unless he does violence to the enemy, his life and that of his family yea even his nation will be in jeopardy.

"For the LORD, the God of Israel, saith that he hateth putting away: for one covereth violence with his garment, saith the LORD of hosts: therefore take heed to your spirit, that ye deal not treacherously." Malachi 2:16

The Sniper is not a sneaky fellow; he is a commissioned soldier by his government to root out, and to pull down, and to destroy, and to throw down, to build, and to plant.
In the life of Jeremiah, we see the making of a Sniper.

"But the LORD said unto me, Say not, I am a child: for thou shalt go to all that I shall send thee, and whatsoever I command thee thou shalt speak. Be not afraid of their faces: for I am with thee to deliver thee, saith the LORD. Then the LORD put forth his hand, and touched my mouth. And the LORD said unto me, Behold, I have put my words in thy mouth. See, I have this day set thee over the nations and over the kingdoms, to root out, and to pull down, and to destroy, and to throw down, to build, and to plant." Jeremiah 1:7-10

God told Jeremiah that He has put words (bullets) in his mouth (barrel) and as he speaks from his heart, triggered by his tongue by faith (the hammer) through his mouth (the barrel) he would root out, pull down, destroy and throw down in the nations. That in a figure is what I am transferring to the USMC Snipers or Navy SEALs around the world as they do service to their nation in times of war.

"And from the days of John the Baptist until now the kingdom of heaven suffereth violence, and the violent take it by force." Matthew 11:12

So, the Sniper is a man/woman who is moved by the violence done against the kingdom of God and with violence takes the enemy out.

"Run ye to and fro through the streets of Jerusalem, and see now, and know, and seek in the broad places thereof, if ye can find a man, if there be any that executeth judgment, that seeketh the truth; and I will pardon it." Jeremiah 5:1

"And judgment is turned away backward, and justice standeth afar off: for truth is fallen in the street, and equity cannot enter.

Yea, truth faileth; and he that departeth from evil maketh himself a prey: and the LORD saw it, and it displeased him that there was no judgment.

And he saw that there was no man, and wondered that there was no intercessor: therefore his arm brought salvation unto him; and his righteousness, it sustained him." Isaiah 59:14-16

Here we see God searching the land looking for a Sniper. So much violence had been done to the people called by the Name of the Lord in the city called by His Name. If there was a Sniper in the land the enemy would not have a foothold in the house of God.

The underground fighters in Poland did much havoc to the Germans during W.W.11. The Sniper makes up the hedge and sets himself up in a strategic position to take out enemies.

The Sniper does not work alone (Matt 8:19). Today there are Sniper helpers with sophisticated binoculars who help in scanning the horizon for the intended target, giving him the coordinates.
Married couples working together in unity ought to be the greatest Snipers. The devil knows this too well and sows seeds of discord in the family.

Anointed to Kill

The Sniper is anointed to kill. He stands as a Watchman, an Intercessor over his family, community, County, State or Nation. He is anointed or licensed to kill. In the movie "The Good the Bad and the Ugly," we see "The Good" is a good shot. He shot the hangman's rope off the neck of the Ugly. As for the end time Sniper, the Spirit of the Lord is upon him, for he has anointed him to snipe at the spirit of poverty so the poor will be poor no more. He shoots at the source of broken heartedness. He shoots down prison doors and shackles, setting the captives free. He lives Isaiah 10:27. He is such a great shot that he can shoot down the strings that bind burdens to one's shoulders and with another shot break the yoke off one's neck.

The whirlwind is a choice weapon for these latter days as we see in
Jeremiah 23:18-20,

"For who hath stood in the counsel of the LORD, and hath perceived and heard his word? who hath marked his word, and heard it? Behold, a whirlwind of the LORD is gone forth in fury, even a grievous whirlwind: it shall fall grievously upon the head of the wicked.

The anger of the LORD shall not return, until he have executed, and till he have performed the thoughts of his heart: in the latter days ye shall consider it perfectly."

The Sniper has a permanent seat at Heaven's Council to receive counsel and appropriate armor for battle. These are the days for the whirlwind of God to go forth for the destruction of the wicked. The time has come for the Prophet-Sniper to arise in this nation and in the nations of the world. He would snipe at abortion doctors, the Congress and Judges that make an unholy decree. Like the two witnesses in the book of Revelation or like Moses and Elijah of old, he would call down fire and hailstones from heaven. He would plague the wicked in this nation just like Moses brought judgment on the Egyptians.

"Thou shalt not suffer a witch to live" Exodus 22:18 is still a valid judgment today for witchcraft. He will call fire on witchcraft covens, burn down their altars and break their cauldrons. He is anointed to bring deliverance to the captives.

"Shall the prey be taken from the mighty, or the lawful captive delivered? But thus saith the LORD, Even the captives of the mighty shall be taken away, and the prey of the terrible shall be delivered: for I will contend with him that contendeth with thee, and I will save thy children. And I will feed them that oppress thee with their own flesh; and they shall be drunken with their own blood, as with sweet wine: and all flesh shall know that I the LORD am thy Saviour and thy Redeemer, the mighty One of Jacob." Isaiah 49:24-26

David literally took a lamb out of a lion's mouth and killed the lion. The same anointing will cause us to be saviors.

Old Testament Snipers

Moses no doubt is my first choice when we come to Snipers in the Old Testament. However, I would like to talk about Joshua first.

*"**Then spake Joshua to the LORD in the day when the LORD delivered up the Amorites before the children of Israel, and he said in the sight of Israel, Sun, stand thou still upon Gibeon; and thou, Moon, in the valley of Ajalon.** And the sun stood still, and the moon stayed, until the people had avenged themselves upon their enemies. Is not this written in the book of Jasher? So the sun stood still in the midst of heaven, and hasted not to go down about a whole day. **And there was no day like that before it or after it, that the LORD hearkened unto the voice of a man: for the LORD fought for Israel.**"* Joshua 10:1-21

What a day to remember in the annals of history. Today, no true calculations can be made concerning the cycle of the earth without taking this day into consideration. Another such event was recorded in Isaiah 38: 1-8. Hezekiah had prayed for more years to be added to his life. God granted his prayer and gave him a sign by dialing back the Sun fifteen degrees. Joshua prayed the Sniper's prayer and God heard and answered speedily.

"Come near, put your feet upon the necks of these kings. And they came near, and put their feet upon the necks of them. And Joshua said unto them, Fear not, nor be dismayed, be strong and of good courage: for thus shall the LORD do to all your enemies against whom ye fight." Joshua 10:24-25

God is waiting on us to make His enemies our footstool. We are also commanded to tread upon serpents, scorpions (demons and witch-doctors); and over all the powers of the enemy. (Luke 10:19)

Moses was a man that knew the ways of God. God's word was in his mouth. In Egypt, by the spoken word he wrought great miracles and brought Israel out of bondage. Moses was a great intercessor and by his prayers the nation was preserved.

"Now the man Moses was very meek, above all the men which were upon the face of the earth." Numbers 12:3

You can see that from his many intercessions for the children of Israel in the Wilderness. When Korah and his company came against Moses, heaven heard his voice and did according to his supplication.

The book of Numbers 16:1-33 is a must read. Moses prayed the Sniper's prayer

"LORD, Respect not thou their offering" **If these men die the common death of all men, or if they be visited after the visitation of all men; then the LORD hath not sent me.** *But if the LORD make a new thing, and the earth open her mouth, and swallow them up, with all that appertain unto them, and they go down quick into the pit; then ye shall understand that these men have provoked the LORD."* Numbers 16:30

1 Kings 8:56 is a testimony of the fulfillment of every word spoken through Moses.

"Blessed be the LORD, that hath given rest unto his people Israel, according to all that he promised: there hath not failed one word of all his good promise, which he promised by the hand of Moses his servant." 1 Kings 8:56

New Testament Sniper's prayers

"And, behold, there came a leper and worshiped him, saying, Lord, if thou wilt, thou canst make me clean." Matthew 8:2

If it be thy will was out of the ignorance of God's willingness. The response of Jesus "I will" should knock out that ignorance today. Also, Peter said *"by whose stripes ye were healed."*

*"**I will** come and heal him."* Matthew 8:5-7

*"My daughter is even now dead: **but come and lay thy hand upon her, and she shall live.** And Jesus arose, and followed him, and so did his disciples."* Matthew 9:18-19

"And, behold, a woman, which was diseased with an issue of blood twelve years, came behind him, and touched the hem of his garment:
*For she said within herself, **If I may but touch his garment, I shall be whole.** But Jesus turned him about, and when he saw her, he said, Daughter, be of good comfort; thy faith hath made thee whole. And the woman was made whole from that hour."* Matthew 9:20-22

"Have mercy on me, O Lord, thou Son of David; my daughter is grievously vexed with a devil….Then Jesus answered and said unto her, O woman, great is thy faith: be it unto thee even as thou wilt. And her daughter was made whole from that very hour." Matthew 15:22-28

"Lord, have mercy on my son: for he is lunatick, and sore vexed: for ofttimes he falleth into the fire, and oft into the water...
And Jesus rebuked the devil; and he departed out of him: and the child was cured from that very hour." Matthew 17:15-18

"Then came to him the mother of Zebedee's children with her sons,

worshipping him, and desiring a certain thing of him.

And he said unto her, What wilt thou? She saith unto him, Grant that these my two sons may sit, the one on thy right hand, and the other on the left, in thy kingdom." Matthew 20:20-22.

This should be an "If it be thy will prayer." It was a good try but God never promised that to her. You cannot demand your daughter's school fees from me if I never promised you.

No rambling, direct to the point, type of prayer is what gets the Lord's attention. The three Hebrew children had no time to ramble before God or King Nebuchadnezzar. If they would pray like many of us today, they would long be dead during the preambles.

"Nebuchadnezzar spake and said unto them, Is it true, O Shadrach, Meshach, and Abednego, do not ye serve my gods, nor worship the golden image which I have set up? **Shadrach, Meshach, and Abednego, answered and said to the king, O Nebuchadnezzar, we are not careful to answer thee in this matter. If it be so, our God whom we serve is able to deliver us from the burning fiery furnace, and he will deliver us out of thine hand, O king.** *Did not we cast three men bound into the midst of the fire? They answered and said unto the king, True, O king.*

He answered and said, Lo, I see four men loose, walking in the midst of the fire, and they have no hurt; and the form of the fourth is like the Son of God. Then Shadrach, Meshach, and Abednego, came forth of the midst of the fire. And the princes, governors, and captains, and the king's counselors, being gathered together, saw these men, upon whose bodies the fire had no power, nor was an hair of their head singed, neither were their coats changed, nor the smell of fire had passed on them. Then Nebuchadnezzar spake, and said, Blessed be the God of Shadrach, Meshach, and Abednego, who hath sent his angel, and delivered his servants." Daniel 3:14-29

This type of praying would bring the Fourth man into your furnace and your life shall be preserved and God will give other men for your life.

Chapter Eight
The Perfect Sniper

Justification: He is born again not of flesh or blood or the will of man but of God. These are the fruits of his recreated spirit:

- Love
- Joy
- Peace
- Longsuffering
- Gentleness
- Goodness
- Faith
- Meekness
- Temperance

When you look at the nine virtues above, can there be any law against any of these?

"And they that are Christ's have crucified the flesh with the affections and lusts." Galatians 5:24

Sanctification: He is wholly separated unto God. He does not conform to this world system. He is a living sacrifice.

The word sanctify is a very interesting one. It implies: being removed from the place of being common and unclean and putting on the nature of God.

The Sniper is in the place of constant communion with God. 1 Thessalonians 5:23

Let us consecrate ourselves absolutely to the working of the Holy Spirit and our sanctification shall be complete.

Holy Ghost Baptism: He is filled with the Holy Ghost and operates the gifts

- Tongues
- Interpretation of Tongues
- Prophecy
- Working of Miracles
- Gift of Faith
- Gifts of Healing
- A word of Wisdom
- A word of Knowledge
- Discerning of Spirits

Spirit of Adoption:

Adoption here is not in the regular sense as we know it but it is the Placement as a Son.

"Now I say, [That] the heir, as long as he is a child, differeth nothing from a servant, though he be lord of all; But is under tutors and governors until the time appointed of the father."
Galatians 4:1-2

In the making of a Priest, you are firstly the son of a High Priest. You must however, meet certain qualifications, be thirty years old and without any deformity to be admitted into the office. Spirit of Adoption is the Spirit of true Sonship and placement as a Son like Jesus. These understand that the Feast of Pentecost and Pentecostalism will not do it. In the Feast of Tabernacles they have their fulfillment.

The Sniper (Son of God) guard's his heart and thought in Christ

Jesus by the peace of God that passes all understanding
   He thinks on whatsoever things that are:

> True,
> Honest,
> Just,
> Pure,
> Lovely,
> Good report;
> Virtuous,
> Praiseworthy.

He is not conformed to this world.

He is transformed by the renewing of his mind, and has proven the good, and acceptable, and perfect, will of God.

He is a carrier of the Christ.

He knows God is able to do exceedingly abundantly above all that he asks or thinks.

He knows that God is working in him both to will and do of His good pleasure.

He is more than a conqueror by the victory of Jesus Christ.

He uses the Name of Jesus Christ with effect.

He knows the meditorial work of Christ and appropriates it.

He meditates in the word day and night.

He practices faith that works by love.

He practices the Word.

He walks in wisdom.

He lives by the bread of heaven.m

He is not ruled by his Senses.

He is called by the Name of the Lord.

He knows in whom he has believed.

He knows no word of God is void of power or fulfillment.

He knows God watches over His Word to perform it.

His Words are spirit and life.

He does nothing of his own accord
He speaks the Father's Words.
He does the Father's Work.
He walks and lives in the spirit.
His way is Love's way.
He is clothed with Glory and Righteousness.
He is Invincible.
He breathes fire and sends Lightning bolts.
He has received the abundance of grace and the gift of righteousness.
He reigns as king in the realms of life.
He is the revelation of Jesus Christ.
He rules over Satan, Principalities, Powers, Rulers of Darkness and Wicked spirits in heavenly places.
He is at rest; perfect peace is his.
He is the stature of a perfect man.
He is a Priest-King after the order of Melchizedek.
He will not taste death.
He is baptized with fire.
His Word (bullet) cannot fail.
He is not anxious.
He by prayer and supplication with thanksgiving makes his request known unto God.
He casts all his cares and anxiety on Jesus.
He knows that God cares for him.
His strength is in quietness and in confidence.
He loves the law and nothing offends him.
He has his mind stayed on the Lord.
He bears the infirmities of the weak.
He is patient and kind.
He is not resentful, nor rude.
He does not rejoice in the wrong but in the right.
He is not jealous, nor boastful.
He has joy unspeakable full of glory.
He does only the things that are pleasing unto God.

His Joy no man takes away.
He rejoices greatly.
His strength is the Joy of Yehovah.
He has obtained gladness and joy, sorrow and weeping fled away.
He knows the path of Life.
He dwells in the presence of God.
He sits at the right hand of God with pleasures forevermore.
He is a fruit bearing branch and his fruit abides.
He is created in righteousness, holiness and truth.
He stands before the Father God without fear or condemnation.
He is the righteousness of God in Christ Jesus.
He is Righteous, Sanctified, Redeemed, and full of Wisdom.
He is able to walk boldly into the throne room of Grace.
He is not a noisy gong or a sounding cymbal.
He is nothing without Love.
He abides in the word and the Word abides in him.
He is God's battle axe and weapon of war.

Chapter Nine
Lessons in Prayer

In recent years, we have seen some unusual type of praying. We have the machine gun type of prayers; also the releasing of heavy curses. A little girl was asked to pray on her 5th birthday and this was how she prayed. "Anyone that says I will not celebrate my 5th birthday, fall down and die." One of my sister's friends was visiting a church and they were told to take their machine guns and begin to shoot at their enemies and the devil. Not to be left out, she corked her hands like a gun and began to shoot "crack ka, ka, ka ka ka, ka." It is laughable and pretty much pathetic. If these groups truly believe their prayers work, why do they have to do it every day for hours and in all night prayers, year in and out? All the wicked, demons and the devil would have been killed a thousand times over and more already. Their lives, Churches and nation should all be glorious. In this type of praying, everybody around you, parents, spouses, siblings is a suspect. Charles G. Finney would not receive prayer from a praying group. He was asked why and his reply was *"You have said with your mouth that your prayers are not answered. It would be a waste of your time, my time and God's time."* (paraphrased)

If you have prayed the same prayers for years without a change, is it not time to find out what works? If I gave you a machine gun with an endless supply of ammunition and you do not know who your enemy is, what is the likelihood you will hit your target? However, if I gave you a small pistol and one bullet and showed you your enemy, are you not more likely to kill your enemy? The subject of prayers is very important and many are praying sincerely to be free from all oppression of the enemy. My prayer is *"May our prayers not be in vain."*

"And in the morning, rising up a great while before day, he went out, and departed into a solitary place, and there prayed. *And he preached in their synagogues throughout all Galilee, and cast out devils."*
Mark 1:32-39

"Then answered Jesus and said unto them, ***Verily, verily, I say unto you, The Son can do nothing of himself, but what he seeth the Father do: for what things soever he doeth, these also doeth the Son likewise.***

For the Father loveth the Son, and sheweth him all things that himself doeth: and he will shew him greater works than these, that ye may marvel. *"*John 5:19-20

"O God, thou art my God; ***early will I seek thee:*** *my soul thirsteth for thee, my flesh longeth for thee in a dry and thirsty land, where no water is; … To see thy power and thy glory, so as I have seen thee in the sanctuary. Because thy lovingkindness is better than life, my lips shall praise thee. Thus will I bless thee while I live: I will lift up my hands in thy name."*Psalms 63:1-4

*"As the hart panteth after the water brooks, so panteth my soul after thee, O God. My soul thirsteth for God, for the living God: when shall I come and appear before God?"*Psalms 42:1-2

Intimacy, fellowship, communion, exaltation of God in prayers is a lost art. All we do today is "give me, give me." Sometimes, we accuse God of withholding blessing and call it wrestling with God in prayer. It is amazing how we demand from God instead of from the devil. We describe how big, awful and terrible the mountain is to God instead of speaking to the mountain. We pray for the things that have been freely given to us. Does anyone lack wisdom? Let him ask, the scripture says. How about peace? *"My peace I give you."*

I have heard people pray and call the name of Satan more than the name of God. Is this praying to God or to Satan? How many of us understand that Satan understands English or the structure of language? Let us take a look at this statement or prayer. *"O God, I command Satan to take his hands off my body."* Who do you think that prayer was addressed to? Is it to God or the devil? It is to God, but why should the devil respond to you then? However, if you said *"Satan, take your hands off my body,"* it would be quite obvious who you are talking to and he has to give you an answer. In the first instance, there is nothing for God to do and since the culprit was not addressed, he cannot respond to you.

Prayer Companions

The Sniper has learned to use what I call prayer companions or prayer combos. Just like bread and butter; bread and egg, bread and fish are combinations, so also prayer has combinations or companions. If you have prayed and you are not getting results, it is time to use these prayer secrets.

"...with fastings and prayers night and day..." Luke 2:37, 5:33

*"…. and in **breaking of bread, and in prayers.**"* Acts 2:42

*"Thy **prayers and thine alms** are come up for a memorial before God."* Acts 10:4

"And at midnight Paul and Silas prayed, and sang praises unto God: and the prisoners heard them." Acts 16:25

"Continue in prayer, and watch in the same with thanksgiving." Colossians 4:2

Praying for others.

*"Always **labouring fervently for you in prayers,** that ye may stand perfect and complete in all the will of God."* Colossians 4:12

*"We give thanks to God always **for you all,** making **mention of you in our prayers.**"* 1 Thessalonians 1:2; Romans 1:9, Romans 15:30, Ephesians 1:16-23, Philemon 1:4, 22

"I exhort therefore, that, first of all, supplications, prayers, intercessions, and giving of thanks, be made for all men;
For kings, and for all that are in authority; that we may lead a quiet and peaceable life in all godliness and honesty.
For this is good and acceptable in the sight of God our Savior;
Who will have all men to be saved, and to come unto the knowledge of the truth." 1 Timothy 2:1-; 2 Timothy 1:3

"For the eyes of the Lord are over the righteous, and his ears are open unto their prayers: but the face of the Lord is against them that do evil." 1 Peter 3:12

"and golden vials full of odors, which are the prayers of saints." Revelation 5:8; Revelation 8:3-4

Liquid Prayers

*"Who in the days of his flesh, when he had offered up **prayers and supplications** with **strong crying and tears** unto him that was able to save him from death, and was heard in that he feared."* Hebrews 5:7; Psalms 39:12

"And I wept much" Revelation 5:4

Tears are liquid prayers that flow to the heart of God. So many years ago when our Son was about 2 years old, one evening, he began to cough. We gave medications and antibiotics to no avail; in fact we had used antibiotics one too many. Each time he coughed, it was as if a dagger pierced my heart. One evening while he was coughing again, I was moved with compassion and tears. I held him up and I told the devil *"Enough !!!; Take your hands off my son"* and immediately he was healed. When you see your child in pain and tears how much can you bear? When he goes beyond cries and tears and begins to groan in pain, every fiber of your being is being torn to shreds. How much more will our heavenly father hear the groaning of the Holy Spirit through us? It is manly to cry before our heavenly father.

During 9/11, I lost so much money in the Stock Market, I was faced with monthly payments of about $7500 and I did not have a dollar but as I flipped the channels, because most were showing planes ramming into the twin towers, I saw Mr. Creflo Dollar. He was preaching about praising God in every situation. With tears in my eyes I stood up and said "Lord, I will praise you anyhow." I praised God with tears and He heard me and began to open doors of favor. A wonderful friend and an in-law wired $10,000.00 to my account without my request. Another friend not knowing came to my house and gave me $500.00; that weekend I did a little job that gave me $900 and within two weeks I had $13,000 in my account.

*"God said to Hezekiah "I have heard thy prayer, I **have seen thy tears:** behold, I will heal thee: on the third day thou shalt go up unto the house of the LORD."* II Kings 20:5.

"Job poured out tears to God." Job 16:20

The father of the epileptic child;

"cried out, and said with tears, Lord, I believe; help thou mine unbelief." Mark 9:24

The woman with the alabaster box wept;

"...and began to wash His feet with tears, and did wipe them with the hairs of her head .." Luke 7:38.

The result was that her sins were forgiven.

The Psalmist declared:

"… put thou my tears into thy bottle: are they not in thy book? When I cry unto thee, then shall mine enemies turn back: this I know; for God is for me." Psalms 56:8-9

Prayer

May God's ear be attentive to your cry and see your tears and answer you speedily and take away every reproach of the enemy.

"They that sow in tears shall reap in joy." Psalms 126:5.

May your Joy be full in Jesus' Name, Amen.

Hindrances to prayers

"… that ye may know the way by which ye must go: for ye have not passed this way heretofore." Joshua 3:3-4

We are called to walk in the spirit and our warfare is not with flesh and blood. God gave us the gift of himself to lead us in the way and we have not availed ourselves of the Holy Spirit our Comforter (Paraclete) - One who is called alongside us to help.

The Holy Spirit witnesses with our spirits and guides us in the way we should walk in. God has an answer to man's inadequacies.

Ignorance versus the Holy Spirit

Darkness - The Spirit enlightens.
Lack of hearing – The Spirit speaks
Remembered not – The Holy Spirit brings to remembrance
Limiting God – The Holy Spirit is the Power of God and nothing shall be impossible with God.
Unbelief – The Spirit of Truth.
Sin – Spirit of Holiness
Fear - Spirit of Boldness
Unrighteousness - Spirit of Righteousness

Neglect or lack of communion with the Holy Spirit is the problem.

"..they rebelled, and vexed his Holy Spirit: therefore he was turned to be their enemy, and he fought against them." Isaiah 63:10

If your defense lawyer or advocate now becomes your enemy you are done for.

"Lack of knowledge will cause us to perish; *"…. and they have **not known my ways**.* "Hebrews 3:10

"…So we see that they could not enter in because of unbelief." Hebrews 3:17-19

Putting boundaries or limitations on God will hinder our prayers.

"…. and limited the Holy One of Israel." Psalms 78:40-41

Not recounting our blessings and past testimonies

*"They **remembered not** his hand, nor the day when he delivered them from the enemy."* Psalms 78:42

Grieving and not securing the help of the Holy Spirit (Paraclete).

".. He maketh intercession for the saints according to the will of God." Romans 8:26-27

Lack of understanding or unity between husband and wife

"… that your prayers be not hindered…" 1 Peter 3:7

Silver Bullets

Hannah had rambled for so many years in prayers without results. The book of James declares:

"Ye lust, and have not: ye kill, and desire to have, and cannot obtain: ye fight and war, yet ye have not, because ye ask not.
Ye ask, and receive not, because ye ask amiss, that ye may consume it upon your lusts." James 4:2-3

This might be your situation, "me!, I!!, myself!!!" It is all about you and your lust. Have you ever thought of the mind of God, His desires, His needs and His wants? If you want healing so that you can feel good, that is a wrong motive in prayers. Healing is not to make you feel good but that the Name of the Lord might be glorified and His Stripes are not in vain. Why do you want to be delivered from the affliction of bareness? So you can be like other women? No, absolute No! It should be for this cause that the word of God cannot fail, bareness is a reproach to the God you serve and His word cannot fail when He said,

"There shall nothing cast their young, nor be barren, in thy land: the number of thy days I will fulfill." Exodus 23:26

God was looking for a Prophet-Priest. The House of Eli had failed God and Hannah was a perfect candidate from the right tribe, but she had not enrolled in the Holy Ghost Sniper's School. She rambled and rambled like a machine gun in prayer without results. The Sniper knows the mind of God and prays it back to Him.

This time around Hannah went to the House of God and prayed the Sniper's prayer.

"And she was in bitterness of soul, and prayed unto the LORD, and wept sore. And she vowed a vow, and said, O LORD of hosts, if thou wilt indeed look on the affliction of thine handmaid, and remember me, and not forget thine handmaid, **but wilt give unto thine handmaid a man child, then I will give him unto the LORD all the days of his life, and there shall no razor come upon his head.***"* 1 Samuel 1:10-11

Her rifle was ready, She prayed from the depth of her being (The hidden man of the heart). She prayed with the Silver bullet;

"give unto thine handmaid a man child, then I will give him unto the LORD all the days of his life, and there shall no razor come upon his head."

She prayed the heart of the Father who was looking for a Prophet-Priest, a prayer that demands attention and brings results. When the Silver bullet (The Father's heart – Word) is in the barrel (mouth), Faiths' hammer is released through the tongue (the trigger) and the Bull's eye is the result. Seek the Silver bullet (God's word, will and heart) and pray it back to Him and the desires of your heart – His desire will find fulfillment.

"and Elkanah knew Hannah his wife; and the LORD remembered her." 1 Samuel 1:19

Abraham, the father of faith said,

"My son, God will provide himself a lamb for a burnt offering: so they went both of them together."
Genesis 22:8

That was a Silver bullet. God made a demand upon Abraham, His covenant partner to offer his son Isaac as a sacrifice. The above statement was in response to this question put forth by his son.

"And Isaac spake unto Abraham his father, and said, My father: and he said, Here am I, my son. And he said, Behold the fire and the wood: but where is the lamb for a burnt offering?" Genesis 22:7

Abraham went ahead according to schedule.
"And the angel of the LORD called unto him out of heaven, and said, Abraham, Abraham: and he said, Here am I.
*And he said, Lay not thine hand upon the lad, neither do thou anything unto him: for now I know that thou fearest God, seeing thou hast not withheld thy son, thine only son from me. And Abraham lifted up his eyes, and looked, and behold behind him a ram caught in a thicket by his horns: and Abraham went and took the ram, and offered him up for a burnt offering in the stead of his son. And Abraham called the name of that place **Jehovah-jireh**: as it is said to this day, **In the mount of the LORD it shall be seen.**"* Genesis 22:9-14

What shall be seen in the mount of the LORD? It is the prophetic word of Abraham *"God will provide himself a lamb."* About 2000 years later, John the Baptist declared of Jesus Christ -

"Behold the Lamb of God, which taketh away the sin of the world." John 1:29

Truly, Jesus Christ became our Paschal lamb sacrificed for us. The book of Hebrews tells us---

"By faith Abraham, when he was tried, offered up Isaac: and he that had received the promises offered up his only begotten son,
Of whom it was said, that in Isaac shall thy seed be called:
Accounting that God was able to raise him up, even from the dead; from whence also he received him in a figure." Hebrews 11:17-19

If we would know the heart of God we would not fear but only believe.
Abraham was willing to give back to God all that he had received from Him, even Isaac.

"If God gave us His Son, will He not also with him freely give us all things?" Romans 8:32

Praying the Heart of God Today

"Christ hath redeemed me from the curse of the law, being made a curse for me: for it is written, Cursed is every one that hangeth on a tree:
That the blessing of Abraham might come on (your name) through Jesus Christ; that I might receive the promise of the Spirit through faith." Galatians 3:13-14

"And if I be Christ's, then am I Abraham's seed, and heirs according to the promise." Galatians 3:29

"Blessed be the God and Father of our Lord Jesus Christ, who hath blessed me with all spiritual blessings in heavenly places in Christ:
According as he hath chosen me in him before the foundation of the

world, that I should be holy and without blame before him in love:
Having predestinated me unto the adoption of a child by Jesus Christ to himself, according to the good pleasure of his will." Ephesians 1:3-5

"I cease not to give thanks, making mention in my prayers;
That the God of my Lord Jesus Christ, the Father of glory, may give unto me the spirit of wisdom and revelation in the knowledge of him:
The eyes of my understanding being enlightened; that I may know what is the hope of his calling, and what the riches of the glory of his inheritance in the saints, And what is the exceeding greatness of his power toward those who believe, according to the working of his mighty power, Which he wrought in Christ, when he raised him from the dead, and set him at his own right hand in the heavenly places,
Far above all principality, and power, and might, and dominion, and every name that is named, not only in this world, but also in that which is to come: And hath put all things under his feet, and gave him to be the head over all things to the church, Which is his body, the fulness of him that filleth all in all." Ephesians 1:16-23 (Adapted)

"For this cause I bow my knees unto the Father of our Lord Jesus Christ, Of whom the whole family in heaven and earth is named,
That he would grant me, according to the riches of his glory, to be strengthened with might by his Spirit in my inner man;
That Christ may dwell in my heart by faith; that I, being rooted and grounded in love, May be able to comprehend with all saints what is the breadth, and length, and depth, and height; And to know the love of Christ, which passeth knowledge, that I might be filled with all the fullness of God. Now unto him that is able to do exceeding abundantly above all that I ask or think, according to the power that worketh in me, Unto him be glory in the church by Christ Jesus throughout all ages, world without end. Amen." Ephesians 3:14-21 (Adapted)

"But what things were gain to me, those I counted loss for Christ.

Yea doubtless, and I count all things but loss for the excellency of the knowledge of Christ Jesus my Lord: for whom I have suffered the loss of all things, and do count them but dung, that I may win Christ,

And be found in him, not having mine own righteousness, which is of the law, but that which is through the faith of Christ, the righteousness which is of God by faith: That I may know him, and the power of his resurrection, and the fellowship of his sufferings, being made conformable unto his death; If by any means I might attain unto the resurrection of the dead. Not as though I had already attained, either were already perfect: but I follow after, if that I may apprehend that for which also I am apprehended of Christ Jesus.

I count not myself to have apprehended: but this one thing I do, forgetting those things which are behind, and reaching forth unto those things which are before, I press toward the mark for the prize of the high calling of God in Christ Jesus." Philippians 3:7-14 (Adapted)

"Be patient therefore, brethren, unto the coming of the Lord. Behold, the husbandman waiteth for the precious fruit of the earth, and hath long patience for it, until he receive the early and latter rain.

Be ye also patient; stablish your hearts: for the coming of the Lord draweth nigh." James 5:7-8

"For this cause I also, since the day we heard it, do not cease to pray for myself, and to desire that I might be filled with the knowledge of your will in all wisdom and spiritual understanding;

That I might walk worthy of the Lord unto all pleasing, being fruitful in every good work, and increasing in the knowledge of God;

Strengthened with all might, according to your glorious power, unto all patience and longsuffering with joyfulness;

Giving thanks unto the Father, which hath made me meet to be partakers of the inheritance of the saints in light:

Who hath delivered me from the power of darkness, and hath translated me into the kingdom of his dear Son:

In whom I have redemption through his blood, even the forgiveness of sins: Who is the image of the invisible God, the firstborn of every creature: For by him were all things created, that are in heaven, and that are in earth, visible and invisible, whether they be thrones, or dominions, or principalities, or powers: all things were created by him, and for him: And he is before all things, and by him all things consist.

And he is the head of the body, the church: who is the beginning, the firstborn from the dead; that in all things he might have the preeminence." Colossians 1:9-18

And the very God of peace sanctify me wholly; and I pray God my whole spirit and soul and body be preserved blameless unto the coming of my Lord Jesus Christ. Faithful is he that has called me, who also will do it." 1 Thessalonians 5:23-24 (Adapted)

"Grace and peace be multiplied unto me through the knowledge of God, and of Jesus my Lord, According as his divine power hath given unto me all things that pertain unto life and godliness, through the knowledge of him that hath called us to glory and virtue: Whereby are given unto me exceeding great and precious promises: that by these ye might be partakers of the divine nature, having escaped the corruption that is in the world through lust. And beside this, giving all diligence, add to your faith virtue; and to virtue knowledge; And to knowledge temperance; and to temperance patience; and to patience godliness; And to godliness brotherly kindness; and to brotherly kindness charity. For if these things be in me, and abound, they make you that ye shall neither be barren nor unfruitful in the knowledge of our Lord Jesus Christ. But he that lacketh these things is blind, and cannot see afar off, and hath forgotten that he was purged from his old sins. Wherefore the rather, I will give diligence to make my calling and election sure: for if I do these things, I shall never fall:

For so an entrance shall be ministered unto me abundantly into the everlasting kingdom of our Lord and Saviour Jesus Christ.

Wherefore I will not be negligent to put always in remembrance these things, that I may be established in the present truth." 2 Peter 1:2-12

• *Let (your name) live, and not die; and let not my men be few.*

• *And this is the blessing of (your name): Hear, LORD, my voice of Praise, and bring me unto my people: let my hands be sufficient for me; and be thou an help to me from my enemies.*

• *And of (your name), Let thy Thummim and thy Urim be with thy holy one, for I have observed thy word, and kept thy covenant.*

I shall teach Jacob thy judgments, and Israel thy law: I shall put incense before thee, and whole burnt sacrifice upon thine altar.

Bless, LORD, my substance, and accept the work of my hands: smite through the loins of them that rise against me, and of them that hate me, that they rise not again.

• *And of (your name), he said, The beloved of the LORD shall dwell in safety by him; and the LORD shall cover him all the day long, and he shall dwell between his shoulders.*

• *And of (your name), he said, Blessed of the LORD be his land, for the precious things of heaven, for the dew, and for the deep that coucheth beneath,*

And for the precious fruits brought forth by the sun, and for the precious things put forth by the moon, And for the chief things of the ancient mountains, and for the precious things of the lasting hills, And for the precious things of the earth and fullness thereof, and for the good will of him that dwelt in the bush: let the blessing come upon the head of Joseph, and upon the top of the head of him that was separated from his brethren.

My glory is like the firstling of his bullock, and his horns are like the horns of unicorns: with them he shall push the people together to the ends of the earth: and they are the ten thousands (your name), and they are the thousands of (your name).

• And of (your name), he said, Rejoice, (your name), in thy going out; and, (your name) in thy tents.

• They shall call the people unto the mountain; there they shall offer sacrifices of righteousness: for they shall suck of the abundance of the seas, and of treasures hid in the sand.

• And of (your name), he said, Blessed be he that enlargeth (your name): he dwelleth as a lion, and teareth the arm with the crown of the head.

And he provided the first part for himself, because there, in a portion of the lawgiver, was he seated; and he came with the heads of the people, he executed the justice of the LORD, and his judgments with Israel.

• And of (your name), he said, (your name) is a lion's whelp: he shall leap from Bashan.

• And of (your name), he said, O (your name), satisfied with favour, and full with the blessing of the LORD: possess thou the west and the south.

• And of (your name), he said, Let (your name) be blessed with children; let him be acceptable to his brethren, and let him dip his foot in oil.

Thy shoes shall be iron and brass; and as thy days, so shall thy strength be. There is none like unto the God of Jeshurun, who rideth *upon the heaven in thy help, and in his excellency on the sky. The eternal God is my refuge, and underneath are the everlasting arms: and he shall thrust out the enemy from before me; and shall say, Destroy them (your name) then shall dwell in safety alone: the fountain of (your name) shall be upon a land of corn and wine; also my heavens shall drop down dew.*

Happy art thou, O (your name): who is like unto thee, O people saved by the LORD, the shield of thy help, and who is the sword of thy excellency! and mine enemies shall be found liars unto me; and I shall tread upon their high places. Deuteronomy 33:29

"Yet it pleased the LORD to bruise him; he hath put him to grief: when thou shalt make his soul an offering for sin, he shall see his seed (your name), he shall prolong his days, and the pleasure of the LORD shall prosper in his hand. He shall see of the travail of his soul, and shall be satisfied: by his knowledge shall my righteous servant justify many; for he shall bear their iniquities." Isaiah 53:8-11

Chapter Ten
Manifestation of the Sons of God

These phrases "*manifestation of the Sons of God; Man-child*" etc. mean many things to many people. Some would at once put a label on anyone that uses such a phrase. There is no doubt many use those high sounding phrases and their lives are not desirable. There are those that have a bloodless religion, the New Age and the likes.

I have met with some well-meaning Christians that say repentance is all we need and they quarrel with the words prosperity, faith, healing and miracles, etc. They are steeped in legalism and frown at miracle ministries. Many such people are plagued by demons and sickness. The point to note is that any truth pushed to an extreme goes off on a tangent, is lopsided, and becomes an error.

When I speak about the Manifestation of the Sons of God, it is not just about supermen but about maturity, righteousness and holiness. It is about putting on or manifesting the character and nature of Jesus Christ of Nazareth.

The purpose of this bride is to bring forth the Man-child – God's Special Forces (144,000)
This bride must be clothed with the sun.

"And there appeared a great wonder in heaven; a woman clothed with the Sun, and the moon under her feet, and upon her head a crown of twelve stars: And she, being with child cried, travailing in birth, and pained to be delivered." Revelation 12:1-2

It is the honor of the sun-clothed woman to bring forth the Man-child.

He was taken from prison and from judgment: and **who shall declare his generation?** *"For he was cut off out of the land of the living: for the transgression of my people was he stricken."* Isaiah 53:8

Who shall declare his generation? This is the big question. In very plain parlance *"who is his seed?"* He was not married and thus did not have an opportunity to have an offspring and as such He is cut off and becomes a curse, dying childless. For this cause my brethren, the word of the Lord in Exodus and Deuteronomy must be doubly fulfilled in the New Testament.

"There shall nothing cast their young, nor be barren, in thy land: the number of thy days I will fulfill." Exodus 23:26

"Thou shalt be blessed above all people: there shall not be male or female barren among you, or among your cattle." Deuteronomy 7:14

This chapter in Isaiah starts with this statement

"Who hath believed our report? And to whom is the arm of the LORD revealed?" Isaiah 53:1

"That it might be fulfilled which was spoken by Esaias the prophet, saying, Himself took our infirmities, and bare our sicknesses."
Matthew 8:17

What He took and what He bore we need not to take nor bear. Rise up and be fruitful in Jesus' Name, Amen.

He shall see His seed

*"Yet it pleased the LORD to bruise him; he hath put him to grief: when thou shalt make his soul an offering for sin, **he shall see his seed**, he shall prolong his days, and the pleasure of the LORD shall prosper in his hand. **He shall see of the travail of his soul**, and shall be satisfied: by his knowledge shall my righteous servant justify many; for he shall bear their iniquities."* Isaiah 53:10-11

The Word of the Lord clearly declares the coming of this righteous seed of Christ, the travail of His soul. They are the precious fruit spoken of in the book of James:

"Be patient therefore, brethren, unto the coming of the Lord. Behold, the husbandman waiteth for the precious fruit of the earth, and hath long patience for it, until he receive the early and latter rain.

Be ye also patient; stablish your hearts: for the coming of the Lord draweth nigh…" James 5:7-8

To be manifested at the end of the age. God sowed an original seed, Jesus Christ, who went ahead and declared:

"Verily, verily, I say unto you, Except a corn of wheat fall into the ground and die, it abideth alone: but if it die, it bringeth forth much fruit." John 12:24

Because of this, there must arise a holy seed of the same nature and character as Jesus Christ at this time. Looking through history, we are yet to see anyone come into this fullness.

"But every man in his own order: Christ the first fruits; afterward they that are Christ's at his coming." 1 Corinthians 15:23

We can rightly say there are two types of Christians in the

world *"the first fruits and others (afterward group)."* Some day I hope to write a book titled, *Rapture: Hoax or Reality?*

Let us begin today to pray and travail like the rest of creation for the time appointed by the Father.

"Now I say, That the heir, as long as he is a child, differeth nothing from a servant, though he be lord of all; But is under tutors and governors until the time appointed of the father." Galatians 4:1-2

"For the earnest expectation of the creature waiteth for the manifestation of the sons of God." Romans 8:19

"For we know that the whole creation groaneth and travaileth in pain together until now. And not only they, but ourselves also, which have the first fruits of the Spirit, even we ourselves groan within ourselves, waiting for the adoption, to wit, the redemption of our body."
Romans 8:22-23

We shall all be changed (metamorphosis). Are you being changed? The butterfly does not emerge from the egg stage, neither from the larva or caterpillar stage. The pupa stage is not an overnight thing but when the day and time appointed by the Father comes, the cocoon breaks and the kingly butterfly emerges. The elect of God, the manifested sons, God's holy priesthood after the order of Melchizedek are in secret preparation now. I pray there will be a holy stirring within the readers of this book to be counted worthy to be part of this holy priesthood. Read my book *There Shall Be A Performance.*

Recently, I asked my wife which way forward. She understood my question. For years different Church leaders and Sects have set dates. 1977 was very prominent, so was 1988. Y2K was a great sales pitch in my opinion. The Red heifer, the Sanhedrin, etc. is being touted around in Judaism and Messianic Christian circles. What is the way forward? Her answer was very simple "intimacy with God." Intimacy with God will never fail.

"The secret of the LORD are with them that fear Him; and He will show them His covenant." Psalms 25:14.

The Antichrist, Sanhedrin, Red heifer will fail but Love never fails.

The new priesthood
(Cessation of oblations and sacrifices by an unholy priesthood)

The new priesthood is a result of the leaven in Pentecost. The sons of Belial have made their way into the old order, bringing shame and reproach to this holy calling. None can take this honor upon themselves except those who are called like Aaron and upon whom the holy anointing oil has been poured. The heart of God in Exodus 19 was to have a kingdom of Priests.

"And ye shall be unto me a kingdom of priests, and an holy nation. These are the words which thou shalt speak unto the children of Israel." Exodus 19:6

But Israel failed in this respect and the tribe of Levi, one of the Children of Jacob on whom was placed the curse; received the priesthood.

"Simeon and Levi are brethren; instruments of cruelty are in their habitations. O my soul, come not thou into their secret; unto their assembly, mine honour, be not thou united: for in their anger they slew a man, and in their self will they digged down a wall.

Cursed be their anger, for it was fierce; and their wrath, for it was cruel: I will divide them in Jacob, and scatter them in Israel."
Genesis 49:5-7

Levi was the only tribe that stood for the Lord in the matter of the golden calf. They refused to join the others in the worship of the golden calf. They were thus inducted into the priesthood. Of old, every man was his own priest. Abel, Noah, and Abraham all offered their own sacrifices. At the Passover it was a priest for a home and here we see a priestly tribe or family for the whole nation.

Just like Levi on whom was put the curse entered the holy priesthood, the people of the "curse" – an unholy priesthood have held the grounds for nearly two thousand years. Some have corrupted themselves like the sons of Eli. As a result, there has to be a change of Priesthood. I have seen Pastors shear the sheep and make fur coats for themselves. As if that was not enough, they used them for barbecue (chopped lamb steak). Their hoofs and horns they polished and used them to decorate their living rooms as trophies of their spoils. So much more can be said of the Evangelists and some self -styled Prophets who prophesy lies to the people. I am not here to castigate my brethren the Priests but to simply state that there is leaven in Pentecost and thus we have an unholy priesthood.

"Bring no more vain oblations; incense is an abomination unto me; the new moons and Sabbaths, the calling of assemblies, I cannot away with; it is iniquity, even the solemn meeting." Isaiah 1:13

It is the heart of God today to begin to pray for the **cessation of oblation and sacrifices by an unholy priesthood** for God is now ready to bring into manifestation a new priesthood.

"And hast made us unto our God kings and priests: and we shall reign on the earth." Revelation 5:10

This is of the stock of Melchizedek not to be counted from the old genealogy but belongs to the New Creation.

"Wherefore, holy brethren, partakers of the heavenly calling, consider the Apostle and High Priest of our profession, Christ Jesus;"
Hebrews 3:1

"So also Christ glorified not himself to be made an high priest; but he that said unto him, Thou art my Son, today have I begotten thee.

As he saith also in another place, Thou art a priest for ever after the order of Melchizedek." Hebrews 5:5-6

"For such an high priest became us, who is holy, harmless, undefiled, separate from sinners, and made higher than the heavens;

Who needeth not daily, as those high priests, to offer up sacrifice, first for his own sins, and then for the people's: for this he did once, when he offered up himself. For the law maketh men high priests which have infirmity; but the word of the oath, which was since the law, maketh the Son, who is consecrated for evermore." Hebrews 7:26-28

"But this man, because he continueth ever, hath an unchangeable priesthood." Hebrews 7:24

The Man-child becomes the first-fruits of this holy and unchangeable priesthood (144,000)

Overshadowing of the Holy Spirit

And in the sixth month the angel Gabriel was sent from God unto a city of Galilee, named Nazareth, To a virgin espoused to a man whose name was Joseph, of the house of David; and the virgin's name was Mary.

And the angel came in unto her, and said, Hail, thou that art highly favoured, the Lord is with thee: blessed art thou among women.

And when she saw him, she was troubled at his saying, and cast in her mind what manner of salutation this should be.

And the angel said unto her, Fear not, Mary: for thou hast found favour with God. And, behold, thou shalt conceive in thy womb, and bring forth a son, and shalt call his name JESUS. He shall be great, and shall be called the Son of the Highest: and the Lord God shall give unto him the throne of his father David: And he shall reign over the house of Jacob forever; and of his kingdom there shall be no end. Then said Mary unto the angel, How shall this be, seeing I know not a man? And the angel answered and said unto her, The Holy Ghost shall come upon thee, and the power of the Highest shall overshadow thee: therefore also that holy thing which shall be born of thee shall be called the Son of God.

And, behold, thy cousin Elisabeth, she hath also conceived a son in her old age: and this is the sixth month with her, who was called barren.

For with God nothing shall be impossible." Luke 1:26-37

Just as Mary brought forth according to the counsel and ordination of the most High God, the Lord Jesus according to the flesh, God is looking for a bride that will bring forth an holy seed, the Man-child at this time. It behooves us to begin to pray this heart of God, the overshadowing of the Holy Spirit upon this virgin church. As we begin to pray this, we will become impregnated by the Holy Spirit and Christ will be formed in us. There is a gestation period after which comes the travail to bring forth.

"Who hath heard such a thing? who hath seen such things? Shall the earth be made to bring forth in one day? or shall a nation be born at once? for as soon as Zion travailed, she brought forth her children.

Shall I bring to the birth, and not cause to bring forth? saith the LORD: shall I cause to bring forth, and shut the womb? saith thy God.

Rejoice ye with Jerusalem, and be glad with her, all ye that love her: rejoice for joy with her, all ye that mourn for her: That ye may suck, and be satisfied with the breasts of her consolations; that ye may milk out, and be delighted with the abundance of her glory." Isaiah 66:8-11

"Oh that thou wouldest rend the heavens, that thou wouldest come down, that the mountains might flow down at thy presence,

As when the melting fire burneth, the fire causeth the waters to boil, to make thy name known to thine adversaries, that the nations may tremble at thy presence! When thou didst terrible things which we looked not for, thou camest down, the mountains flowed down at thy presence."

Isaiah 64:1-3

"Blessed be the LORD my strength, which teacheth my hands to war, and my fingers to fight: My goodness, and my fortress; my high tower, and my deliverer; my shield, and he in whom I trust; who subdueth my people under me. LORD, what is man, that thou takest knowledge of him! or the son of man, that thou makest account of him! Man is like to vanity: his days are as a shadow that passeth away.

Bow thy heavens, O LORD, and come down: touch the mountains, and they shall smoke. *Cast forth lightning, and scatter them: shoot out thine arrows, and destroy them. Send thine hand from above; rid me, and deliver me out of great waters, from the hand of strange children;*

Whose mouth speaketh vanity, and their right hand is a right hand of falsehood. I will sing a new song unto thee, O God: upon a psaltery and an instrument of ten strings will I sing praises unto thee.

It is he that giveth salvation unto kings: who delivereth David his servant from the hurtful sword. Rid me, and deliver me from the hand of strange children, whose mouth speaketh vanity, and their right hand is a right hand of falsehood: That our sons may be as plants grown up in their youth; that our daughters may be as corner stones, polished after the similitude of a palace: That our garners may be full, affording all manner of store: that our sheep may bring forth thousands and ten thousands in our streets: That our oxen may be strong to labour; that there be no breaking in, nor going out; that there be no complaining in our streets. Happy is that people, that is

in such a case: yea, happy is that people, whose God is the LORD."
Psalms 144:1-15

Church without spot or wrinkle

"That he might present it to himself a glorious church, not having spot, or wrinkle, or any such thing; but that it should be holy and without blemish." Ephesians 5:27

Spot relates to stain, sin. Satan and angels of light come with shining garments but to the student of the word they easily detect the spot in his garment. The leaven of Pentecost that has been in the Church for about two thousand years cannot go beyond the Day of Atonement. I have heard well-meaning, fleshly but ignorant men say "we cannot be holy in this earthly realm until we get to heaven." They are making void the word of God. The scriptures are very plain *"Let God be true and every man a liar."* Wrinkle relates to pressure but blessed be God who declares that we are like Mount Zion that cannot be moved. God's commands *"Be ye holy"* -- *"Be ye perfect"* are not vain talk but a demand by a Holy God. *"Run that you may obtain."*

A crown awaits individuals who win. It is an individual race; do not follow the herd. Pay the price for *"mastery."*

The clothing of the bride

"I saw the Holy City, the new Jerusalem, coming down out of heaven
from God, prepared as a bride adorned for her husband."
Revelation 21:2

*"For he hath clothed me with **the garmemts of salvation**, he hath covered me with **the robe of righteousness**, as a bridegroom decketh himself with ornaments, and as a **bride adorneth herself with her jewels**."* Isaiah 61:10

"As the bridegroom rejoiceth over the bride, so shall thy God rejoice

over thee." Isaiah 62:5

*"Can a maid forget her **ornaments**, or a bride her **attire**? yet my people have forgotten me days without number."* Jeremiah 2:32

"For thus saith the LORD of hosts, the God of Israel; Behold, I will cause to cease out of this place in your eyes, and in your days, the voice of mirth, and the voice of gladness, the voice of the bridegroom, and the voice of the bride. Wherefore hath the LORD pronounced all this great evil against us? Or what is our iniquity? Or what is our sin that we have committed against the LORD our God? Because your fathers have forsaken me, saith the LORD, and have walked after other gods, and have served them, and have worshipped them, and have forsaken me, and have not kept my law; And ye have done worse than your fathers; for, behold, ye walk every one after the imagination of his evil heart, that they may not hearken unto me: Therefore will I cast you out of this land into a land that ye know not, neither ye nor your fathers; and there shall ye serve other gods day and night; where I will not shew you favor." Jeremiah 16:9-13

"And there came unto me one of the seven angels which had the seven vials full of the seven last plagues, and talked with me, saying, Come hither, I will shew thee the bride, the Lamb's wife." Revelation 21:9

The bride makes herself ready. A promissory note was given at the introduction of the bride and bridegroom, and that He would surely come again with the full payment. He loved the Church and gave His life for her. On the day of Pentecost, He came with a token, which is the promissory note. He will surely come and redeem it with the full payment. All through history especially through the Church ages, we see how the bride became so complacent and misplaced her ornament and today she is nothing but a whore reveling in drunkenness and all abominable acts. Today, statistics show there is more divorce in the "Church" than in the world. Worse still, there are more abortions among Pentecostal girls than among other denominations. Yet Pentecostals pride themselves as the bride of Christ. Many Pentecostals today do not even speak in other tongues. A very well known Pentecostal denomination agrees that only about 40% of their congregation have the Baptism of the Holy Spirit. A few operate the gifts of the Holy Spirit but a vast majority know nothing about the fruit of the spirit which is the true ornament of the bride of Christ.

"Because thou sayest, I am rich, and increased with goods, and have need of nothing; and knowest not that thou art wretched, and miserable, and poor, and blind, and naked:I counsel thee to buy of me gold tried in the fire, that thou mayest be rich; and white raiment, that thou mayest be clothed, and that the shame of thy nakedness do not appear; and anoint thine eyes with eyesalve, that thou mayest see." Revelation 3:14-18

The nation that truly typifies this spirit is the USA and rightly a great Prophet of God by the name of William Marrion Branham once had a vision of a parade before a grandstand. Each nation marched past and when it came to the turn of the USA, they were stark naked dancing to the tune of rock n' roll. That is the state of Pentecostalism today. Just like God took Abraham out of the Ur of Chaldees to make a new nation out of him, God also separated Hannah so that she might bring forth a new priesthood unto Him. God is reaching out to a bride that He will endow with the Spirit of travailing and prevailing prayers, that would truly pray the heart of God and give him a Man-child. It was only when Hannah vowed a child unto God, meeting the demand of God for a son to replace the House of Eli that her request was granted. God is looking for that Church or people where-so-ever they may be, who will begin to cry out like Hannah. They will be the sun clothed woman in Revelation Chapter 12. The bride truly makes herself ready by putting embroidery on her linen to beautify it for her wedding day.

Today's Pentecostals dress to "kill" and are very sensual without the spirit. The Apostle Peter rightly said,

"Whose adorning let it not be that outward adorning of plaiting the hair, and of wearing of gold, or of putting on of apparel;

But let it be the hidden man of the heart, in that which is not corruptible, even the ornament of a meek and quiet spirit, which is in the sight of God of great price. For after this manner in the old time the holy women also, who trusted in God, adorned themselves, being in subjection unto their own husbands." 1 Peter 3:3-5

"For they shall be an ornament of grace unto thy head, and chains about thy neck." Proverbs 1:9

Sister Chameleon wears red hair, red bag, red shoes, very tight red dress and red earrings to the morning service and at the evening service what do you think she wears? She goes to her wardrobe with shades of colors more than the rainbow and spends hours thinking about combinations, permutations and probabilities, most probably weeks ahead. I believe in prosperity and decency in clothing but if you are caught in such a situation you definitely need deliverance. The true bride of Christ will not need to rush to a designer's wardrobe when the bridegroom comes. They might be at the mill grinding, at the river washing their clothes but their spirits are clothed, waiting and saying "Come Lord Jesus, come."

The Sniper as a good soldier will not be entangled by the daughters of Cain.

It must be noted again that many gallant soldiers did not die on the battlefields but on the laps of a Delilah. Pentecostalism is very heavily infested by the daughters of Cain today. However, like Jezebel of old, all painted up was eaten up by dogs, the same judgment awaits these. Blessed are those who are properly clothed with the ornament of meekness.

"I will greatly rejoice in the LORD, my soul shall be joyful in my God; for he hath clothed me with the garments of salvation, he hath covered me with the robe of righteousness, as a bridegroom decketh himself with ornaments, and as a bride adorneth herself with her jewels."
Isaiah 61:10

What would your attitude be to your betrothed wife if while you were gone she finds pleasure in other men? She does not mourn your absence and her eyes are not piercing the distant road looking for the soon appearing of her bridegroom? In the story of the prodigal son, we see the intense longing of the Father for his son.

"But when he was yet a great way off, his father saw him, and had compassion, and ran, and fell on his neck, and kissed him." Luke 15:20

Are you passionately waiting for him? Listen to this unfortunate story: A man had waited many years to get himself a bride. After the wedding, the bridegroom who came from a distant land across the ocean started putting the paperwork together to get the bride across. The day finally came and the bride came. With great joy the bridegroom welcomed her with great excitement that his lonely and longing heart would be satisfied. Granted, the lady suffered from jet lag, but jet lag does not last for 7 months. The man comes home from work with great expectation that his bride would be at the door to welcome him. The bride is asleep. He wakes up the bride and her response is "I do not like being disturbed when I'm asleep." I was invited to preach at the welcoming party and my sermon was seen by many as inappropriate. The title of my message was *Leprosy in the House*.
I took my text from Leviticus 14:34-45

"When ye be come into the land of Canaan, which I give to you for a possession, and I put the plague of leprosy in a house of the land of your possession;......Then the priest shall come and look, and, behold, if the plague be spread in the house, it is a fretting leprosy in the house: it is unclean. And he shall break down the house, the stones of it, and the timber thereof, and all the morter of the house; and he shall carry them forth out of the city into an unclean place."
Leviticus 14:34-45

The message was a warning to the new couple and the older ones too. As at the time of this writing, the house is ready to be torn down.

So many years ago, a White couple came to me requesting I conduct a marriage ceremony for them. I requested a counseling session with them which took about two hours or more. In the process, I told the groom it was important to pray and seek counsel before marriage so you do not marry a woman whose grandmother died of cancer, her mother died of cancer and she too has cancer. Furthermore, during my inquiry I found out that she was Catholic and I asked her if she was "born again." I explained what it meant and gave her an opportunity to give her life to Christ and let all the reproach of yesterday be gone. She refused and I bid them goodbye. The groom later told me that she got mad at him in the car, accusing him of telling me the details of her life. Her grandmother and mother died of cancer and she had been diagnosed with cancer. The unfortunate thing was that the groom had lost his previous wife to cancer and was now marrying into another "cancer" family. They got themselves another minister who performed the marriage ceremony. The"Church today who claims to be the bride of Christ is unclean and has a festering leprosy. The death spirit of cancer is working in the "Church." God must bring out a bride that He would covenant with and come with the circumcision of the heart at this end time. It is our duty to begin to pray for her. Pray for the "Agnes of God."

The Sniper that Never Was

Elijah was a Sniper and he mentored Elisha, a Sniper in his own right. However, Gehazi the servant of Elisha became "*The Sniper That Never Was.*" We would presume he dealt faithfully until Naaman the Syrian General, a leper, came at the instance of a slave girl to be healed of his leprosy. The prophet sent a messenger to Naaman to dip Seven times in the Jordan River for his cleansing. After much displeasure he did what he was instructed to do and he was made whole. He then offered money and raiment to Elisha. Elisha would not take any gift from the General. Greed and covetousness entered into Gehazi and he ran after the General and with a cock and bull story, extracted raiment and money from the General. After hiding the stuff,

"…he went in, and stood before his master. And Elisha said unto him, Whence comest thou, Gehazi? And he said, Thy servant went no whither.

And he said unto him, Went not mine heart with thee, when the man turned again from his chariot to meet thee? Is it a time to receive money, and to receive garments, and Olive yards, and vineyards, and sheep, and oxen, and menservants, and maidservants? The leprosy therefore of Naaman shall cleave unto thee, and unto thy seed forever. And he went out from his presence a leper as white as snow." 2 Kings 5:25-27

What an unfortunate way to end his career. He had seen the miracle of the Shunamite woman having a child and the raising of the child from the dead. He was probably a witness to Elisha smiting the Syrian army with blindness. His eyes were opened to see the chariots of fire. Despite all the manifestations that he saw with his own eyes from the ringside--- *"and he went out from his presence a leper as white as snow."* If you see a Jewish man today with leprosy that has passed from generation to generation he might well be the offspring of Gehazi, the Sniper that never was. How many Prophets run today greedily after gains like Balaam?

David cried *"how are the mighty fallen!"* 2 Samuel 1:19

"How are the mighty fallen in the midst of the battle! O Jonathan, thou wast slain in thine high places. I am distressed for thee, my brother Jonathan: very pleasant hast thou been unto me: thy love to me was wonderful, passing the love of women. How are the mighty fallen, and the weapons of war perished!" 2 Samuel 1:25-27

"Ye mountains of Gilboa, let there be no dew, neither let there be rain, upon you, nor fields of offerings." 2 Samuel 1:21

Jonathan was a great warrior and he preferred David and they became covenant brothers. There is no doubt whatsoever in my mind that he would have become David's right-hand man in the Kingdom.

Years later -

"David said, Is there yet any that is left of the house of Saul, that I may shew him kindness for Jonathan's sake? And Ziba said unto the king, Jonathan hath yet a son, which is lame on his feet. And the king said unto him, Where is he? Then king David sent, and fetched him out of the house of Machir, the son of Ammiel, from Lo'debar. And David said unto him, Fear not: for I will surely shew thee kindness for Jonathan thy father's sake, and will restore thee all the land of Saul thy father; and thou shalt eat bread at my table continually. Then the king called to Ziba, Saul's servant, and said unto him, I have given unto thy master's son all that pertained to Saul and to all his house." 2 Samuel 9:1-9

Now is the time to thresh down every mountain of Gilboa

Behold, I will make thee a new sharp threshing instrument having teeth: thou shalt thresh the mountains, and beat them small, and shalt make the hills as chaff. Isaiah 41:15 (Jeremiah 51:33; Micah 4:13; Habakkuk 3:12-13)

Do not miss out on this high calling but confront every giant and every mount as we move to the righteous side with God. Every mountain must be pulled down and every valley filled.

Chapter Eleven
Prayerlessness

Prayerlessness is lack of vital and conscious union with God.

Prayerlessness is:
Lack of communion with God.
Preferring sleep more than praying.
Fasting without praying.
Leaving the home without praying.
Eating before remembering to pray.
Doing stuff without first praying.
Marrying without praying.
Sleeping without praying.
Waking without praying.
Not withdrawing from activities to spend time in prayer.
Not keeping quiet to hear from God.
Rambling words before God.
Asking amiss in prayer.
Not being precise or definite in prayer.
Unbelief in prayer.
Not prevailing in prayer.
Not travailing in prayer.
Not spending time in prayer (In and Out or Drive through praying).
Not giving the best time to prayers.
Not giving thanks in prayers.
Regarding iniquity and praying.
Preaching without praying.

Hearing the Word without praying for effect.
Fighting in the flesh instead of praying.
Complacency instead of praying.
Selfishness in prayer, me, I, myself, Amen.
Doing religious activities instead of praying.
Not praying for the peace of Jerusalem.
Not praying the heart and mind of the Father God.
Evidenced by divorce (spiritual and physical).
Evidenced by death (spiritual and physical).
Evidenced by lack.
Evidenced by lack of breakthrough.
Evidenced by spiritual stagnation.
Evidenced by lack of Love.
Evidenced by lack of Joy.
Evidenced by lack of Peace.
Evidenced by lack of Patience.

Chapter Twelve
The Eyes of a Sniper

I had spoken earlier on that the Sniper has 20/20 vision. In Sniper training they actually require 20/40 and 20/70 vision in one eye. The Sniper's telescope is well adjusted and the night is as the day because of his night vision equipment. I would like us to dwell more on this aspect of Spiritual sight. Blindness is a great malady and in a very strange way there are more physically blind and lame people among the other religions especially among the Muslim world. The reason should be plain. They have refused Jesus Christ, the light of the world and so they suffer both spiritual and physical blindness.

There is a popular saying among the tribe of my origin "*If one is blind, beauty is gone.*" Let us apply this to Spiritual blindness. If one is spiritually blind, the beauty of the Supernatural, the miraculous realm, the essence of Christianity is gone. Blindness in the "Church" world is so predominant that the sayings of old "*if the blind lead the blind they will both fall into the pit*" holds true in this generation more than ever before. The Christian, the bible says is the light of the world but they have become as spiritually dense and become a black hole, like the world and have no light to give. If the light in you is darkness - "*how great is the darkness,*' the scripture says. Jesus Christ came that those who seat in darkness might have light. However, we who are called the light of the world and a leader of the blind have lost sight and thus like the salt, it is good for nothing —"*but to be trodden under foot by men.*"

Balaam's Donkey

"And the ass saw the angel of the LORD standing in the way, and his sword drawn in his hand: and the ass turned aside out of the way, and went into the field: and Balaam smote the ass, to turn her into the way." Numbers 22:23

Balaam's donkey has more spiritual insight than many church leaders and folks today. In India so many years ago, someone rightly observed that before one of the many devastating earthquakes that hit India, the cows that were resting by the wall for shade moved away to the open field. The birds stopped chirping and the fishes would not bite. Man was totally indifferent, insensitive or more so, spiritually blind and some took the spaces made vacant by the animals to rest under the shade as a canopy. Then, suddenly, the earthquake came and many lives were lost and men were crushed under this wall. In the Tsunami story in Thailand, we all heard on the news that the animals moved to higher grounds but what happened to the natural man? They were eating, drinking, playing, getting married and having the pleasures of life. Some were swimming nude on the beaches and suddenly this great destruction came. It was a great deluge like in the days of Noah. The media described it as "destruction of biblical proportion." If we assume that the rest of the world is blinded because the prince of this world hath blinded the eyes of those that believe not, what about the believers? Where were the Priests and Pastors and all them that put on a religious garb? They were supposed to be light and they were supposed to warn the people. Noah cried out loud for 120 years. If one would have cried out loud even for 120 minutes, there would have been no lives lost. Here we see that not only the unbelievers perished but many "Christians" too. If you are a Pastor and you could not warn some of your congregation who went for vacation of impending danger, then you are as spiritually blind as Balaam was and it is time for the donkeys to take your place. Many of us preachers today are like

Balaam running after the gold and the silver and devising many ways to take money from people and thus, have become blinded by riches.

"Which have forsaken the right way, and are gone astray, following the way of Balaam the son of Bosor, who loved the wages of unrighteousness;" 2 Peter 2:15; Jude 1:11; Revelation 2:14.

See if these sound familiar to you? *"God is going to raise five Millionaires in this Church and I would like you to step out with a seed of $10,000 dollars; God has given me a word for you I feel led to tell you to sow a faith seed that would really stretch you for $1,000 dollars; There is something about a $1000 seed; I have traced out my right-hand on paper; I want you to place your hand in it in agreement and mail it back to me with a seed of $1000, $500, or $100;*
I have anointed green prayer cloth or green olive oil from the Holy land and I will send it in the mail when you send us your prayer request with a gift of $100."

It is possible that some of these preachers once had spiritual sight but are now choked or blinded by the cares of this world. They have lost their sight and have become *"blind as a bat"* but many follow them and would perish with them except of course if they seek the truth for themselves. The mercy of God never runs out until our time runs out—for it is appointed unto men, once to die but after this, the judgment, (Hebrews: 9.27). This is the biggest problem with the Laodicean Church Age which we represent. They claim they see but God's assessment or judgment is different.

*"Because thou sayest, I am rich, and increased with goods, and have need of nothing; and knowest not that thou art wretched, and miserable, and poor, and **blind**, and naked..... and **anoint thine eyes with eyesalve, that thou mayest see**.*" Revelation 3:14-18

Once, a smallish Prophet came from California to Phoenix Arizona.

He said "Someone is going to sow a seed of $100,000 and a special blessing is awaiting the person." A lady stood up to receive the paper slip. The prophet felt if the lady stood up to give $100,000, there must be more where the money came from. He asked the lady's hand in marriage and she declined. The lady decided to give the $100,000 to a Charity instead.

This brings me to the different categories of blindness:

There are those who are totally blind physically like Bartimaeus and thus have no light at all who wear the garment of blindness, carrying a cane. This ought to depict the unbelieving world but unfortunately it is the precarious situation of the generality of the "Church" today having a form of godliness but denying the power thereof. These have not received the glorious light of the gospel. The needed prayer is to rip off the veil of blindness, bind the devil and claim their salvation and deliverance and ask God to send someone to harvest them into the kingdom. However, most Christians though born- again have never seen any glimmer of light and thus have been blinded and veiled at birth. No one taught them that at birth their spirit was quickened and thus alive to the realities of the supernatural realm. Unlike the first generation of Christians, we have made them-- **twice the children of hell.**

There are those like the man Jesus prayed for and said "*he saw men like trees walking*" and thus needed the second touch. Many such are in the Church today especially in the Prophetic Movement and running with the little light but it is very obvious they need the second touch so they can rightly say "I can see." I am not here to castigate this movement.

It is a great Movement however, because it is borne out of Pentecost. It has leaven in it. Leaven is sin – imperfection. Unless they are willing to move to the next level – The Feast of Tabernacles, The feast of Fullness where no leaven is found, they would be onlookers like the sons of the prophets (School of the Prophets) in the days of Elijah/Elisha when the Elijah Saints come on the scene.

Some once saw the light, walked in the light but as they organized and became denominational echoes, blindness started setting in and today in relation to Laodicea we have total eclipse. They are veiled; of such we have men like Gehazi, Balaam and Hymaneus (having loved this present world). Some are blinded by their denominational zeal like Saul of Tarsus and say the days of miracles are gone and others yet say *"we are it and no one else."* God's judgment of Laodicea is very simple *"that thou art wretched, and miserable, and poor, and **blind**, and naked:"*

There are those who see now but they realize that it must be progressive and like the Apostle Paul they want to apprehend that for which they have been apprehended.

This last category is the Sniper category. They have good sight but are not satisfied until their darkness is like the noon day Sun in its strength. Nothing will be hidden from them. God will not hide anything from them. To Abraham, God said:

"Shall I hide from Abraham that thing which I do;
Seeing that Abraham shall surely become a great and mighty nation and all the nations of the earth shall be blessed in him?" Genesis 18:17-18

These prayers of Paul are their hearts' cry until they reach full manifestation as the apprehended ones.

"… may give unto you the spirit of wisdom and revelation in the knowledge of him: The eyes of your understanding being enlightened; that ye may know what is the hope of his calling, and what the riches of the glory of his inheritance in the saints, And what is the exceeding greatness of his power to us-ward who believe, according to the working of his mighty power." Ephesians 1:17-23

These prayers are for those who are called to this high calling and are pressing on to apprehend it. They enter into the rest spoken of in the book of Hebrews. They would have deep inward sight into spiritual things and be able to communicate the same and thus will truly be God's light in this present darkness.

In relation to the man that was born blind we see Jesus said:

"As long as I am in the world, I am the light of the world." John 9:5

This statement was preceded by the words

"I must work the works of him that sent me, while it is day: the night cometh, when no man can work." John 9:4

It is time to work and be proof producers so that the world might know that Jesus Christ is the same yesterday, today and forevermore and He is still in the world today.

It is time for spit and mud again. Lord, anoint my eyes with this mixture so I can see and let the religious world begin to argue *"…is he the man that was born blind?"* Some would say *"…he looks like him."* One thing is certain, just like that man, you have your testimony.

"Then again the Pharisees also asked him how he had received his sight. He said unto them, He put clay upon mine eyes, and I washed, and do see." John 9:15

"One thing I know, that, whereas I was blind, now I see." John 9:25

We, can like Jesus say

"Verily, verily, I say unto you, The Son can do nothing of himself,

*but what he **seeth** the Father do: for what things soever he doeth, these also doeth the Son likewise."* John 5:19

This is very significant and must be prayed through by those who will apprehend the call to be Snipers for Jesus *"what he **seeth** the Father do."* Unless we can see the Father or pierce the veil into the supernatural realm, the greater works spoken by Jesus cannot be. When you begin to see ear drums and brand new hearts through your spiritual telescopic sight or you see cancer or tumors disappearing, you pull the trigger, faith goes into action to release the word and you can rightly say *"Thus saith the Lord"* This was very characteristic of the ministry of William Marrion Branham.

I will be writing more about this fore-runner ministry. Prophets of biblical proportions are going to rise very shortly who by their works, will begin to shake nations.

Let us look at the account of Jeroboam sending his wife to the prophet, Ahijah.

"And Jeroboam said to his wife, Arise, I pray thee, and disguise thyself, that thou be not known to be the wife of Jeroboam… and go to him: he shall tell thee what shall become of the child.

"… But Ahijah could not see; for his eyes were set by reason of his age.

And the LORD said unto Ahijah, Behold, the wife of Jeroboam cometh to ask a thing of thee for her son; for he is sick: thus and thus shalt thou say unto her: for it shall be, when she cometh in, that she shall feign herself to be another woman. And it was so, when Ahijah heard the sound of her feet, as she came in at the door, that he said, Come in, thou wife of Jeroboam; why feignest thou thyself to be another? for I am sent to thee with heavy tidings." I Kings 14:2-6

The thing to note is that the prophet had become physically blind by reason of age and the woman also disguised herself. The scripture rightly says *"there is nothing hidden that will not be brought to light.*" When these end-time Prophets come on the scene, secret sins will be laid bare. Elijah was not there when Jezebel schemed to kill Naboth in order for Ahab to possess Naboth's vineyard but he showed up with a declaration of, "*Thus saith the Lord.*"

The cry of the King in that instance was--"*Hast thou found me, my enemy?*" You cannot hide from God or from His Sons.

"Looking unto Jesus the author and finisher of our faith; who for the joy that was set before him endured the cross, despising the shame, and is set down at the right hand of the throne of God." Hebrews 12:2

Jesus saw something; as a result he is set down at the right hand of Majesty. Balaam did not see until God opened his eyes. God is the only one that gives sight to the blind. We see Jesus in the New Testament giving sight to the blind. He does not only heal the physically blind but gives sight to those who are spiritually blind. The scriptures say "*the people who sat in darkness have seen a great light.*" Matthew 4:16. Jesus said, "*I am the light of the world.*" He is the light that lights the path of every man that comes into the world. God is light and in Him is no darkness at all. The Snipers are the light of the world.

The Eyes of a Sniper versus The Eyes of the Wicked

"And he said, Go, and tell this people, Hear ye indeed, but understand not; and see ye indeed, but perceive not. Make the heart of this people fat, and make their ears heavy, and shut their eyes; lest they see with their eyes, and hear with their ears, and understand with their heart, and convert, and be healed." Isaiah 6:9-10

"And the disciples came, and said unto him, Why speakest thou

unto them in parables? He answered and said unto them, Because it is given unto you to know the mysteries of the kingdom of heaven, but to them it is not given. For whosoever hath, to him shall be given, and he shall have more abundance: but whosoever hath not, from him shall be taken away even that he hath. Therefore speak I to them in parables: because they seeing see not; and hearing they hear not, neither do they understand. And in them is fulfilled the prophecy of Esaias, which saith, By hearing ye shall hear, and shall not understand; and seeing ye shall see, and shall not perceive: For this people's heart is waxed gross, and their ears are dull of hearing, and their eyes they have closed; lest at any time they should see with their eyes, and hear with their ears, and should understand with their heart, and should be converted, and I should heal them. But blessed are your eyes, for they see: and your ears, for they hear. For verily I say unto you, That many prophets and righteous men have desired to see those things which ye see, and have not seen them; and to hear those things which ye hear, and have not heard them." Matthew 13:10-17

"(According as it is written, God hath given them the spirit of slumber, eyes that they should not see, and ears that they should not hear) unto this day." Romans 11:8

"The eyes of your understanding being enlightened; that ye may know what is the hope of his calling, and what the riches of the glory of his inheritance in the saints," Ephesians 1:18

"Having eyes full of adultery, and that cannot cease from sin; beguiling unstable souls: an heart they have exercised with covetous practices; cursed children:" 2 Peter 2:14

"The Spirit of the Lord is upon me, because he hath anointed me to preach the gospel to the poor; he hath sent me to heal the brokenhearted, to preach deliverance to the captives, and recovering of sight to the blind, to set at liberty them that are bruised,
To preach the acceptable year of the Lord." Luke 4:18-19

"Open thou mine eyes, that I may behold wondrous things out of thy law." Psalms 119:18

"They have mouths, but they speak not: eyes have they, but they see not:
They have ears, but they hear not: noses have they, but they smell not:
They have hands, but they handle not: feet have they, but they walk not: neither speak they through their throat. They that make them are like unto them; so is every one that trusteth in them." Psalms 115:5-8

"But if our gospel be hid, it is hid to them that are lost: In whom the god of this world hath blinded the minds of them which believe not, lest the light of the glorious gospel of Christ, who is the image of God, should shine unto them." 2 Corinthians 4:3-4

"I will lift up mine eyes unto the hills, from whence cometh my help."
Psalms 121:1

"Unto thee lift I up mine eyes, O thou that dwellest in the heavens.
Behold, as the eyes of servants look unto the hand of their masters, and as the eyes of a maiden unto the hand of her mistress; so our eyes wait upon the LORD our God, until that he have mercy upon us."
Psalms 123:1-2

"But strong meat belongeth to them that are of full age, even those who by reason of use have their senses exercised to discern both good and evil." Hebrews 5:14

What is your Christian goal? Someone once asked me and my response was to be like Jesus. To be conformed to His very image so that as He is, so am I in this world. For many, their goal is heaven. God's provided way to become like Jesus is so simple and yet so sublime. "See Jesus!"

See Jesus

*"… **Sir, we would see Jesus.** Philip cometh and telleth Andrew: and again Andrew and Philip tell Jesus. And Jesus answered them, saying, The hour is come, that the Son of man should be glorified. Verily, verily, I say unto you, Except a corn of wheat fall into the ground and die, it abideth alone: but if it die, it bringeth forth much fruit. He that loveth his life shall lose it; and he that hateth his life in this world shall keep it unto life eternal. If any man serve me, let him follow me; and where I am, there shall also my servant be: if any man serve me, him will my Father honour."* John 12:20-26

I pray that this request by the Greeks *"**Sir, we would see Jesus**"* would be your heart's cry and ambition. I believe what I am about to reveal is one of the greatest keys in the New Testament. Jesus was simply pointing to a futuristic event that would come about as a consequence of Him, the corn of wheat dying and bringing forth many Jesuses just like Himself. Isaiah the Prophet asked a very pertinent question -

"Who shall declare His generation?" He continued *"when thou shalt make his soul an offering for sin, he shall see his seed, he shall prolong his days; He shall see of the travail of his soul, and shall be satisfied."* Isaiah 53:10-11

Dr. James went on to tell us about the precious fruit of the earth. The precious fruit is the first fruit which belongs to the Lord and is offered unto Him in the Old Testament. Today many pastors clamor for the first fruit to be given to them. Some churches demand your pay slip or stubs to determine if you are paying the right amount of tithe. It is all about the gold, and paying for the upkeep of their airplanes.

"Be patient therefore, brethren, unto the coming of the Lord. Behold, the husbandman waiteth for the precious fruit of the earth, and hath long patience for it, until he receive the early and latter rain.

Be ye also patient; stablish your hearts: for the coming of the Lord draweth nigh." James 5:7-8

The "Rapture" has been wildly and widely preached, but no one gives you the conditions or qualifications for the *"Rapture."* Someday I will be writing a book titled, "Rapture, Hoax or Reality?" Therein, I will be talking about the pros and cons which are the general beliefs about it and proceed to reveal the third side of the coin, that which has eternal value. I put the word *"Rapture"* in quote because there is so much falsehood attached to it. One thing is certain ---we shall all be changed.

The word "changed" is the Greek word metamorphoo from where we derived the English word metamorphosis

"But we all, with open face beholding as in a glass the glory of the Lord, are **changed** *into the same image from glory to glory, even as by the Spirit of the Lord."* 2 Corinthians 3:18

Many of us have seen metamorphosis play out before us as kids in grade or elementary schools. For our son David, he had this experiment done in First grade. The teacher brought a larvae to the classroom. They fed it leaves and it went through the different stages. One day, the cocoon broke and there came out a lovely Monarch Butterfly. Why many in Christendom today, even many in the End-time ministries believe a sudden anointing would fall on them at the sound of a trumpet and they would fly away no matter how or what stage they are in, beats my imagination hollow and overwhelms me. The sounding of the trumpet only activates the cocoon to break open or to be made manifest. There is no doubt a waiting period even in the cocoon stage and if I may add, it is not every cocoon that brings forth. Some die and do not come to manifestation. I am almost getting too excited and spilling too much. The key thing here according to the scriptures is that as we behold the glory of the Lord, so shall we go through the transfiguration and transformation from one stage to another.

*"For God, who commanded the light to shine out of darkness, hath shined in our hearts, to give **the light of the knowledge of the glory of God in the face of Jesus Christ.** But we have this treasure in earthen vessels, that the excellency of the power may be of God, and not of us."*
2 Corinthians 4:6-7

The light of this knowledge is only as we see Jesus.

"While we look not at the things which are seen, but at the things which are not seen: for the things which are seen are temporal; but the things which are not seen are eternal." 2 Corinthians 4:18

*"But rejoice, inasmuch as ye are partakers of Christ's sufferings; that, **when his glory shall be revealed**, ye may be glad also with exceeding joy."* 1 Peter 4:13

*We have also a more sure word of prophecy; whereunto ye do well that ye take heed, as unto a light that shineth in a dark place, **until the day dawn, and the day star** arise in your hearts:* 2 Pet 1:19

*"That the trial of your faith, being much more precious than of gold that perisheth, though it be tried with fire, might be found unto praise and honour and glory **at the appearing of Jesus Christ:**"* 1 Peter 1:7

"Beloved, now are we the sons of God, and it doth not yet appear

*what we shall be: but we know that, **when he shall appear**, we shall be like him; **for we shall see him as he is**.* "I Joh n 3:2

Only those that have been granted the grace to see will see and thus be changed.

I would wish to reiterate these facts:

Spiritual sight is the doorway into the supernatural and miracles.

What we see we become.

When we truly see, there is no haggling over doctrines.

He that sees does not stumble.

*"But if the ministration of death, written and engraven in stones, was glorious, so that the children of Israel could not steadfastly behold the face of Moses for the glory of his countenance; which glory was to be done away: How shall not the ministration of the spirit be rather glorious? For if the ministration of condemnation be glory, much more doth the ministration of righteousness exceed in glory. For even that which was made glorious had no glory in this respect, by reason of the glory that excelleth. For if that which is done away was glorious, much more that which remaineth is glorious. Seeing then that we have such hope, we use great plainness of speech: And not as Moses, which put a vail over his face, that the children of Israel could not stedfastly look to the end of that which is abolished: But their minds were blinded: for until this day remaineth the same veil untaken away in the reading of the old testament; which veil is done away in Christ. But even unto this day, when Moses is read, the veil is upon their heart. Nevertheless when it shall turn to the Lord, the veil shall be taken away. Now the Lord is that Spirit: and where the Spirit of the Lord is, there is liberty. But we all, with open face beholding as in a glass the glory of the Lord, are **changed** into the same image from glory to glory, even as by the Spirit of the Lord."* 2 Corinthians 3:7-18

I would like to leave you these scriptures for your meditation.

"Wherefore he saith, Awake thou that sleepest, and arise from the dead, and Christ shall give thee light." Ephesians 5:14

"Awake to righteousness, and sin not; for some have not the knowledge of God: I speak this to your shame." 1 Corinthians 15:34

"Thy dead men shall live, together with my dead body shall they arise. Awake and sing, ye that dwell in dust: for thy dew is as the dew of herbs, and the earth shall cast out the dead." Isaiah 26:19

"Arise, shine; for thy light is come, and the glory of the LORD is risen upon thee. For, behold, the darkness shall cover the earth, and gross darkness the people: but the LORD shall arise upon thee, and his glory shall be seen upon thee." Isaiah 60:1-2

"The sun shall be no more thy light by day; neither for brightness shall the moon give light unto thee: but the LORD shall be unto thee an everlasting light, and thy God thy glory. Thy sun shall no more go down; neither shall thy moon withdraw itself: for the LORD shall be thine everlasting light, and the days of thy mourning shall be ended. Thy people also shall be all righteous: they shall inherit the land for ever, the branch of my planting, the work of my hands, that I may be glorified. A little one shall become a thousand, and a small one a strong nation: I the LORD will hasten it in his time." Isaiah 60:19-22

"At midday, O king, I saw in the way a light from heaven, above the brightness of the sun, shining round about me and them which journeyed with me. And when we were all fallen to the earth, I heard a voice speaking unto me, and saying in the Hebrew tongue, Saul, Saul, why persecutest thou me? it is hard for thee to kick against the pricks.

And I said, Who art thou, Lord? And he said, I am Jesus whom thou persecutest. But rise, and stand upon thy feet: for I have appeared unto thee for this purpose, to make thee a minister and a witness both of these things which thou hast seen, and of those things in the which

I will appear unto thee; Delivering thee from the people, and from the Gentiles, unto whom now I send thee, **To open their eyes, and to turn them from darkness to light, and from the power of Satan unto God, that they may receive forgiveness of sins, and inheritance among them which are sanctified by faith that is in me.** *Whereupon, O king Agrippa, I was not disobedient unto the heavenly vision:"* Acts 26:13-19

I feel impressed like Peter to write the same thing again unto you, for repetition is needful here.

Except we see Jesus, the (change) metamorphosis will not take place and it is from glory to glory until the breaking forth. As we see Jesus (revelation) in His many facets, so do we become like Him. The picture of the chameleon comes to view, that changes according to what it sees. The chameleon generally has negative connotation however, this change is not transient but a real transfiguration. As we see Him clothed in righteousness we must change into that very image. He then shows us another facet and we are transformed until for the last time so to speak when we see Him we are just like Him for as He is so are we.

"And he said unto them, Go ye, and tell that fox, Behold, I cast out devils, and I do cures **to day and tomorrow, and the third day** *I shall be perfected."* Luke 13:32

Let us **See** today, tomorrow (from glory unto glory) and the third day we shall be perfected.

Let them who have eyes to see, See.

William Marrion Branham was truly a Prophet-Sniper sent from God. There has been no man since the days of the Apostles who has exhibited such a phenomenal walk with God. His gift of the word of wisdom and word of knowledge were at one hundred percent accuracy. Not one word of his has fallen to the ground. He was an example of a true Sniper of the 20th century. However, unlike Elijah who mentored Elisha, he did not raise up a successor or disciple. Rather, what we have seen are Sniper impersonators. It would do us good to read a large number of the visions that he put out in his day--- perhaps, it would elicit a hunger in our hearts. It is my belief that he was more like John the Baptist, a forerunner of an end-time move. He spoke about the Third Pull, where there would be no impersonators. Amongst other things, he declared that when the prophet and the prophetic generations come on the scene, they would be totally vindicated by God. When that time comes, the voice of the prophet which declares –"Thus saith the Lord" will reverberate again and silence all the naysayers. This would be a voice ordained by heaven which would make all that is false and counterfeit manifest in that day. A cursory look at everything that has come to pass shows that he spoke with authority. Concerning Jesus, we are told:

"For he taught them as one having authority, and not as the scribes." Matthew 7:29

Baptism of Fire

The Sniper has received the baptism of fire; as such he is clothed with fire.

He has been purified like the sons of Levi. Every iota of dross has been burnt away. He now truly reflects the heavenly image upon whom the departed glory is restored. Like the three Hebrew children, natural fires, even atomic fire cannot kindle upon them. The purpose of purging or purification like silver is to reflect the image of Jesus, the refiner of silver.

He has been transfigured into the self-same image as the Master.

He is a kindler of fire wherever he goes. Fires proceed out of his mouth to devour his enemies. Wings of fire lick sickness and diseases leaving them neither root nor residue. Fiery wheels move them about at the speed of light. Travels to distant lands and tribes are in a twinkle. What a wonder to put on a glorified body.

"*Life and death are in his tongue, he can kill and make alive (raise the dead)*" Proverbs 18:21

Being born again is the awakening of our spiritual sight. The Eunuch who worked under Candace the Queen read the book of Isaiah. He was captivated by what he read and he needed help for a deeper understanding. By a miracle of transportation, Philip was sent to him to help him. He was a worthy seeker and those who truly hunger and seek shall have their eyes opened. Phillip opened the scriptures and the man saw Jesus and his response was, "*This is water. Why can't I be baptized now?*" Can I enter into that covenant now? He did and so can you. You are born-again, but it is the beginning of the race you must run. The field or track you are on is not familiar grounds or territory. It would appear as if you have to blaze it alone but you are really not alone. This is the role of the Holy Spirit and He is your guide. He is not a blind leader of the blind. No human being can take you through this path, they can only point the way by their lives and testimonies. The Holy Spirit knows the way through this wilderness and His work according to Jesus is to "*take of me and shew it unto you.*" Will you let Him do his work or have you relegated his role to tongues only? He can only show you through your spiritual eyes being enlightened. So, we must see at our spiritual birth. We must continue to see with the Holy Ghost baptism until we see Him as He is which culminates in the blowing of the trumpets signifying the beginning of the Feast of Tabernacles. Gehazi saw, but was blinded by riches. The knowledge of seeing into the supernatural, the chariots of fire, horses, and warring angels ready to battle with flaming swords of vengeance should have made Gehazi or whoever was the servant of Elisha tremble and desire a quadruple anointing.

There is coming, a seven fold anointing on the elect of God, the Sons of God, the End-time Snipers. There shall be an awesome display of God's power before the close of this age. Get ready, get ready.

There will be testing and trials. Get ready to pass the exams.

"There hath no temptation taken you but such as is common to man: but God is faithful, who will not suffer you to be tempted above that ye are able; but will with the temptation also make a way to escape, that ye may be able to bear it. Wherefore, my dearly beloved, flee from idolatry." 1 Corinthians 10:13-14

To you my brethren let the word "Mahanim" take a hold in our lives. It means - we have company.

"But ye are come unto mount Sion, and unto the city of the living God, the heavenly Jerusalem, and to an innumerable company of angels," Hebrews 12:22

Jacob wrestled with an angel and he asked for a blessing and his name was changed. God will appear to our enemies to rebuke them like he did to Laban on behalf of Jacob or to false prophets or witch doctors like Balaam *"you cannot curse but bless."* We have the ministry of angels and those who have eyes will see them ministering alongside the heirs of salvation.

Paul saw and his life was forever impacted just like John in the Island of Patmos who saw the glory of the Lord. Peter, James and John at the Mount of Transfiguration saw the glory of the Lord. Peter referred to it thus:

"For we have not followed cunningly devised fables, when we made known unto you the power and coming of our Lord Jesus Christ, but were eyewitnesses of his majesty. For he received from God the Father honour and glory, when there came such a voice to him from the excellent glory, This is my beloved Son, in whom I am well pleased.

And this voice which came from heaven we heard, when we were with him in the holy mount." 2 Peter 1:16-18

From John we read:

"That which was from the beginning, which we have heard, which we have seen with our eyes, which we have looked upon, and our hands have handled, of the Word of life; (For the life was manifested, and we have seen it, and bear witness, and shew unto you that eternal life, which was with the Father, and was manifested unto us;)" I John 1:1-2

Isaiah was a man of visions; the Prophet Ezekiel saw supernatural lights. Jeremiah was asked, *"What seest thou?"*

"Moreover the word of the LORD came unto me, saying, Jeremiah, what seest thou? And I said, I see a rod of an almond tree.
Then said the LORD unto me, Thou hast well seen: for I will hasten my word to perform it." Jeremiah 1:11-12

The same question *"what seest thou?"*---was posed to Amos and Zechariah and the same question is being posed to us today. *"What seest thou?"* What is your response? *"I am blind. I cannot see; I see men like trees"* or would you like Eli say *"my eyes are dim"* or can you rightly speak forth what you see? I pray the words spoken to Jeremiah the Prophet will resound in our ears *"Thou hast well seen."*

The Ministry of Angels

Angels have been known even in modern times to be involved in battles against Israel's enemies. The actions of angels in the Old Testament are well documented. The ministry of angels in the New Testament should be evident today. For these are the days of the New Testament and as we enter into the last days of this age with all the woes, vials and trumpets that are to be released by the ministry of angels, it really is amazing that we have neglected such a ministry.

"Are they not all ministering spirits, sent forth to minister for them who shall be heirs of salvation?" Hebrew 1:14

"Therefore we ought to give the more earnest heed to the things which we have heard, lest at any time we should let them slip." Hebrews 2:1

We have let slip this day the ministry of angels but not so those who are called to be Snipers. They have to depend on the ministry of angels.

"And it came to pass, when I, even I Daniel, had seen the vision, and sought for the meaning, then, behold, there stood before me as the appearance of a man. And I heard a man's voice between the banks of Ulai, which called, and said, Gabriel, make this man to understand the vision." Daniel 8:15-16

Angels come as men. Angel Gabriel was sent to make Daniel understand the vision. As the Snipers begin to seek to understand the times and the seasons, God will send Gabriel to His own to give them understanding. There would be resistance by principalities but Prince Michael would be unveiled to battle through on our behalf. Angels are designated to do specific jobs. In the ministry of William Branham there was an angel involved in his healing ministry. Many have questioned it and spoken without understanding.

"Now there is at Jerusalem by the sheep market a pool, which is called in the Hebrew tongue Bethesda, having five porches.
In these lay a great multitude of impotent folk, of blind, halt, withered, waiting for the moving of the water. For an angel went down at a certain season into the pool, and troubled the water: whosoever then first after the troubling of the water stepped in was

made whole of whatsoever disease he had." John 5:2-4

This angel no doubt is a healing angel and since Jesus has come, is he now jobless? If this is true, then it must also mean that, since the Holy Spirit has come, Jesus no longer has a role to play. God is God and He has organizational structures and job descriptions.

"Bless the LORD, ye his angels that excel in strength, that do his commandments, hearkening unto the voice of his word." Psalms 103:20

There are financial angels, warrior angels, and security or protection angels. They respond to the Word. If there are dark clouds over a city or heaven is like brass, it is because principalities, hosts of wickedness are in operation. However, when Snipers appear, the power of God begins to manifest. There shall be war in the heavens and the wicked ones would be crushed. The man-child would arise and they would take their place in the heavenlies. Archangel Michael and his angels would arise to do battle with the devil and his hosts and no place would be found for them any more in the second heaven and they will be made manifest on the earth and woe unto them who do not have the whole armor of God on and cannot come and go to the Capital glory realm and appear before the throne room of grace.

Jesus Christ said,

"Verily, verily, I say unto you, Hereafter ye shall see heaven open, and the angels of God ascending and descending upon the Son of man." John 1:51

This is the fulfillment of Jacob's ladder--

"And he dreamed, and behold a ladder set up on the earth, and the top of it reached to heaven: and behold the angels of God ascending

and descending on it." Genesis 28:12

It is declaring unto us an open heaven and the ministry of angels.

Angels strengthen, and for those who say we got the Holy Ghost and we do not need the ministry of angels: Did the Holy Spirit come upon Jesus? So what are you going to do with these scriptures?

"Then the devil leaveth him, and, behold, angels came and ministered unto him." Matthew 4:11

"And there appeared an angel unto him from heaven, strengthening him." Luke 22:43

"Also I say unto you, whosoever shall confess me before men, him shall the Son of man also confess before the angels of God:" Luke 12:8

When you pray to the Father and make declarations concerning the word, Jesus will repeat it before the angels and they would go forth to bring it about.

Chapter Thirteen
Hitting the Bull's Eye

It is very strange that everyone acknowledges a problem but no one offers a solution. It is important we know how to get results or how things work and work it out. There are three things we must be proficient in as Snipers: Word, Faith and Prayers.

God gave man His Word to rule by. It is of primary importance that we give the Word of God first place in our lives. The Word is absolute and it is the law that governs and keeps the universe. Adam and Eve became naked without the Word.

Forever O Lord thy word is settled.

The Word cannot fail.

The Word is God's messenger.

The Word is yea and Amen.

Thy Word is truth.

The Word creates and upholds all things.

Faith is a declaration of "thy word is truth."

Faith never contradicts the Word of God.

Faith is an absolute trust in the Word (promises of God). It is God's ability to make good and deliver on His promises.

Faith is calling into existence that which does not exist.

Faith plus the Word gives the desired result.

Faith is being fixed, unshaken, unmovable. It is the offering of thanksgiving and giving glory to God that the task has been accomplished.

Faith is appropriating the blessings of Abraham.

Faith is the substance ..... My simple revelation of this scripture is "Faith is the original stem cell that produces the things desired."

We walk by faith and not by sight. This implies circumstances are not the evidence. This brings to mind the words of Smith Wigglesworth the Apostle of Faith, "I am not moved by what I see, I am not moved by what I feel, I am only moved by the word of God." Abram did not consider his body nor yet the deadness of Sarah's womb. It is very important to note that the arm of flesh or senses (symptoms) will fail you and dig you deeper in trouble. It is a curse to do so. We will remember the Name of the Lord.

Supplication: - The release of a specific favor or grace. The blind man asked for Mercy. Jesus said what grace do you want? 'That I might receive my sight' was his response and that was the favor he got.

*"Praying always with all **prayer and supplication in the Spirit**, and watching thereunto with all perseverance and **supplication for all saints**;"* Ephesians 6:18

There are different types of prayers. Prayer A will not work for a situation when you need to pray; Prayer B. Praying amiss implies you cannot hit the bull's eye no matter how much you try. Some in what they think is a show of humility say *"If it be thy will or thy will be done"* this is for a different type of prayer, a prayer of commitment or dedication.

Let us use Eph 6:18 type of praying: Prayer firstly is communion with God. You begin by gaining access. You cannot use your key without the door. Prayer is intimacy with God, loving Him. Supplication is asking Him to be favorably disposed to you, asking for a specific grace. This is done by praying in the Holy Ghost (praying in tongues). And as you wait for the desired result, do not fail to ask the same favor for other Christians you know who need the same thing. A wonderful woman of God carried a tumor for some years. She prayed about her situation and prayed for many others with similar tumors. One day a woman came to her with the same type of tumor, as she laid hands on her and commanded the tumor to leave, they were both healed simultaneously.

Some people have no right using Phillipians 4:16 in prayers. You can only lay claim on that if you did what the Phillipians did. You may only lay claim on Luke 6:38, *"give and it shall be given to you,"* based on the measure you have given. One time I prayed for an asthmatic lady many times without result. When I had knowledge that it was a witchcraft attack, I revoked the curse and she was healed.

In praying, find out what scriptures you need to use for the specific situation; what type of Prayer you need and meet the requirements. Commune with God, be specific, and stand on God's faithfulness and giving thanks.

Fear and worry will rob us of peace and victory in our prayers. It is important to follow God's prescription. He cannot do what He has put in your hands to do. You have no right to carry what He has carried for you or go digging for the seed you committed to the earth. Two scriptures must be ingrained in us:

*"**Be careful for nothing**; but in everything by prayer and supplication with thanksgiving let your requests be made known unto God."* Philippians 4:6

"Casting all your cares upon him; for he careth for you." 1 Peter 5:7

We all need to have a time and a date on record that we settled this account (of casting all our cares, worries and anxieties) with God. And remind fear, worry and care when the account was settled. Luke 12:22 says not to bring it to your thought and that means, do not meditate on it. We need to submit, surrender and cast all our cares on the Lord, and then and only then, can we truly resist the devil. We thus can tell the devil to talk to our Lawyer and Advocate, because the case is in His hands. What are the things freely given unto us? – Power, love and a sound mind 11Tim. 1:7. Peace – My peace I give you. Faith – the measure of faith. God's Testament and will for our lives are-- Healing, prosperity and blessings.

Once again, there are rules that govern prayers and when we lay them down exactly, we hit the bull's eye one hundred percent, every time.

The primary purpose and work of the Devil is to steal (to take away from you that which is legally and rightfully yours), kill (to snuff out life, breath as doth a python a prey) and destroy (to annihilate, change the original state).

You are God's victorious Holy Ghost Invasion Sniper Corp; born to win at the end of this age.

Chapter Fourteen
God's Special Forces

The USA has a great military force, divided into four branches, namely:

The Army, the Air force, the Marines and the Navy.

The Army has six Special Forces two of note are the Green Beret and Delta Force.

The Air Force has the Air Force Special Operations Command (AFSOC) and its appendages the 16th SOW, 352nd SOG, 353rd SOG, 720th STG, 18th FLTS, 919th SOW and the 193rd SOW.

The Marines Special Force is known as U.S.M.C Force Recon.

The Navy has U.S. Navy Special Operations that comprises the Seals and the Special Boat Units. (From their various websites)

These are highly specialized and trained individuals with a great commission to protect America, Americans and fight enemies of America wherever they are found. My special interest in these groups are the skills they possess, the training they go through, sometimes beyond human endurance and their willingness to lay down their lives for their nation.

When I think of young Marines some 18, 19 years old who shed their blood in battlefields around the world, my heart bleeds and I salute their courage.

I salute the courage of all American Forces that have died, are wounded or maimed in the defense of the United States of America. These men and women put to shame many modern day Christians who do not even know the great price paid for their freedom.

The Navy Seals

These are Special Forces, consisting of one to six men, usually involved in covert operation. You can call them the Mighty Atom. The name SEAL is derived from their area of operations Sea-Air-Land. It brings to mind an old song that says *"On the mountain, in the valley, on the land and in the Sea ..."* God is God over the Sea, Air and Land. Victory is assured in every battlefield of life both in the natural and the supernatural.

Navy SEALs like other Special Forces are involved in Counterterrorism, Direct Action, Foreign Internal defense (specialty of Green Beret), Special Reconnaissance and Unconventional Warfare. There are never dull moments for a SEAL. He is either on a mission or in constant training getting ready for one.

To become a Navy Seal is no easy task. Paul the Apostle in talking about Christian discipline and endurance compared it to an athlete training for the Olympics to get a wreath of flowers. If Paul were in our age, I have no doubt whatsoever in my mind that he would have compared the victorious Christian and an overcomer to a Navy SEAL receiving the Trident pin.

Navy Seal training is very rigorous, brutal and almost beyond human endurance. Is there any wonder they graduate only about 25% of their intakes? The scripture talks about resistance unto blood. They are trained in extremes of weather and conditions they are likely to operate under for about thirty months. One very important lesson honed down their psyche is the word *"teamwork."* The bible greatly emphasizes teamwork comparing it to the functioning of the physical body. This lesson has not been learnt yet in this generation looking for superstars, people whom they also worship. Every Navy SEAL is a superstar in his own right yet plays his given role in full cooperation in the team. It is important to note that officers and enlisted men compete for placement in the Navy SEAL. God is looking for Ministers and laymen that would qualify for a place in God's Special Forces. The goal of a Master in the East is for his disciples or students to be like him and even bigger. Jesus was wholly clear on this subject. (John 14:12-14) He did not rebuke Peter for wanting to walk on water. He rebuked the disciples when they could not heal the epileptic child, (Matthew 17:14-17).

He literally was saying *"How long am I going to be the only Superstar? Disciples, when are you going to start doing the works that I do?"* So many years ago, I was talking to a very young enthusiastic man about the simplicity of the gospel. He was caught up in a group that cooks up mysteries. I prayed for his healing and was going to teach him how he could pray and grow out limbs. His response amazed me, "No, no, don't make common what Evangelist, (also called the Prophet) does." I told him healing should be common and actually Jesus called it the children's bread. I am glad I wrote the book *Healing!!! The Children's Bread.* Many have stunted their spiritual growth as they look on those with ministerial gifts as superstars and themselves as bench warmers. Good news folks! In the military, the nomenclature (rank) does not matter when competing for a position as a Navy SEAL; an officer, petty officer or private first class, can all compete. However, according to www.howstuffworks.com, they must meet the initial requirements listed below:

Be an active –duty member of the U.S Navy

Be a man

Be 28 or younger

Have good vision – 20/40 in one eye and 20/70 in the other

Be a U.S citizen

Pass the Armed Services Vocational Aptitude Battery (ASVAB)

Pass a stringent physical screening test that includes the following procedure:

Swim 500 yards in 12.5 minutes or less, followed by a 10-minute rest

Perform 42 push-ups in under two minutes, followed by a two minute rest

Perform 50 sit-ups in under two minutes, followed by a two minute rest

Perform six pull-ups, followed by a 10-minute rest

Run 1.5 miles in boots and long pants in less than 11.5 minutes

Once the basic requirements listed above are met, real training begins in earnest. It is called Basic Underwater Demolition/SEAL (BUS/S) Training. This training is divided into four phases, (www.howstuffworks.com):

Indoctrination

Basic Conditioning

SCUBA training

Land-warfare training

Indoctrination is a very powerful force and has been used by the Communists, Fascists and some Religious groups as an evil tool of destruction. Someday, very soon shall appear the Manifested Sons of God, God's Navy SEALs, highly indoctrinated with the doctrine of the Christ. They shall be filled with all the fullness of God. (Ephesians 3:19) As a stone cut without hand they shall smite the kingdoms of this world and establish the Kingdom of Christ. Moses knew the ways of God, but for these young men, indoctrination was the time they inculcated in them the ways and expectation of a Seal.

It has never ceased to amaze me when some celebrity gets born-again; he or she is soon paraded over television and becomes a preacher overnight without meeting any basic requirements. I know many preachers today who should be sitting in a 3rd grade Sunday school class.

Basic Conditioning

This is when the going gets tough and only the tough get going. During this phase, many give up and drop out of the program Drop on Request (DOR). *"No man after laying hold on the plough* -(Luke 9:62).

However, many are called but few are chosen. (Matthew 22:14).

This phase involves running, swimming, tough obstacle courses, calisthenics etc. All these are timed events and the expectations must be met. They go through surf torture at temperatures between 65and 68 degrees Fahrenheit (18-20) degrees centigrade, and are then required to run a mile or two soaking wet, boots and all and sometimes, carrying their rubber boats and they move from one task to another. Part of their swimming training requires their hands and feet tied to carry out some feats in a 9ft deep pool. They also carry out one to two miles Ocean swim.

All these are yet the beginning of "sorrows" as they are yet to go through the infamous Hell Week. The Hell Week is the time to go through sleep deprivation for five and a half days with continuous training. It is at this point many give up. They are actually pushed beyond human endurance. Those who endure to the end shall be saved the scripture declares. (Matthew 24:13). How I wish leaders of the Apostolic and Prophetic movements would take an excursion to the Naval Seal training base during this period. They should stay up and watch these young men overcome. We know nothing about suffering with Christ but we want to reign with Him.

We must remember the acronym Sea-Air-Land (SEAL). They operate in the sea and scuba training-- underwater demolition expertise requirement is a must. The land warfare involves weapon training, handling explosives, hand combat, survival skills and many others. The survivors of the Hell Week proceed to the Advanced Navy Seal Training which takes care of the "Air" part of the Acronym. The parachute training is at the Army Airborne School, Fort Benning, GA.

This training is followed by SEAL Qualification Training (SQT). It is another 15 Weeks of training where they improve on their skills and learn new techniques. It is after all these they are presented with their Naval Enlisted Code and the well-earned SEAL Trident pin. Hooyah!!

It is to be remembered that a SEAL is either involved in missions or in continuous practice getting ready for one.

Every Preacher and Church folks should appreciate the making of a SEAL and ask one question. If these young men would go through these gruesome, beyond human endurance training for the nation America, what am I willing to do for the Kingdom of God?

I salute every Navy Seal; your hard work and devotion dwarfs and eclipses my work and devotion to God. I am highly encouraged and challenged by your mental and physical aptitude and fire in your guts, to press on for the utmost of God that it would be said of me "Fire in his bones" or "God's nuclear reactor." Hallelujah!!

God's Special Forces shall be men:

Filled with power from on high

Filled with all the fullness of God

Who know the price and value of their lives

Who know who they are

Who talk like God

Fight like God

Reign as God on the earth.

There is the call of God to live in holiness, righteousness and power. We are not alone; God's grace is our sufficiency.

We have the ministry of angels to help us and above all the Holy Spirit indwells us. One angel killed 185,000 Assyrian soldiers. Herod the king died as a result of a slight touch from an angel and one angel will bind Satan and throw him into the Lake of Fire.

David's mighty men were truly "Navy SEALs" The three men that fetched water from the well of Bethlehem were amazing. 2 Sam 23:15, 16. May we say Hooyah or rather Hallelujahs to every command of God.

A day of reckoning is at hand. If Paul the great Apostle with all his credentials truly deserving of heaven's Trident pin said *"lest I be a castaway"* what will happen to those who are at ease in Zion? There are missionaries paying the price in China and other parts of the world, truly carrying the Cross of Christ.

All I can say is "O Lord, have mercy upon us"

I would like to close with this word of God to me and for you.

"The price for my life was the life of God, and the value of my life is God."

Chapter Fifteen
Prayers in the Bible

That thine eyes may be open toward this house night and day, even toward the place of which thou hast said, My name shall be there: *that thou mayest hearken unto the prayer ..*

*And hearken thou to the **supplication** of thy servant, and of thy people Israel.... **and when thou hearest, forgive.***

*If any man trespass against his neighbour, and an oath be laid upon him to cause him to swear, and the oath come **before thine altar in this house:***

Then hear thou in heaven, and do, and judge thy servants, condemning the wicked, to bring his way upon his head; and justifying the righteous, to give him according to his righteousness.

*When thy people Israel be smitten down before the enemy, because they have sinned against thee, **and shall turn again to thee, and confess thy name, and pray, and make supplication unto thee in this house:***

Then hear thou in heaven, and forgive the sin of thy people Israel ...

*When heaven is shut up, and there is no rain, because they have sinned against thee; **if they pray toward this place, and confess thy name, and turn from their sin,** when thou afflictest them:* I Kings 8:28-35

*"Then **hear thou in heaven,** and forgive the sin of thy servants,... **and give rain upon thy land, which thou hast given to thy people for an inheritance.***

*…and **spread forth his hands toward this house:***
*but cometh out of a far country **for thy name's sake;***
***(For they shall hear of thy great name, and of thy strong
hand, and of thy stretched out arm;)** …and do according to all
that the stranger calleth to thee for: **that all people of the earth
may know thy name, to fear thee, as do thy people Israel; and
that they may know that this house, which I have builded, is
called by thy name.***

*"If thy people go out to battle against their enemy, whithersoever
thou shalt send them, and shall pray unto the LORD toward the city
which thou hast chosen, and toward the house that I have built for
thy name:*
*Then hear thou in heaven their prayer and their supplication, and
maintain their cause."* I King 8:36-45

*"If they sin against thee, (for there is no man that sinneth not,)…
and **repent, and make supplication** unto thee …*
***And so return unto thee with all their heart, and with all
their soul, in the land of their enemies, which led them away
captive, and pray unto thee toward their land, which thou
gavest unto their fathers, the city which thou hast chosen, and
the house which I have built for thy name:** Then **hear thou** their
prayer and their supplication in heaven thy dwelling place ….**That
thine eyes may be open unto the supplication of thy servant,
and unto the supplication** of thy people Israel, to hearken unto
them in all that they call for unto thee… he arose from before the
altar of the LORD, **from kneeling on his knees with his hands
spread up to heaven.**"* I King 8:46-54

*"And the LORD appeared to Solomon by night, and said unto
him, **I have heard thy prayer, and have chosen this place to
myself for an house of sacrifice. If my people, which are called
by my name, shall humble themselves, and pray, and seek my
face, and turn from their wicked ways; then will I hear from
heaven, and will forgive their sin, and will heal their land.***

Now mine eyes shall be open, and mine ears attend unto the prayer that is made in this place. For now have I chosen and sanctified this house that my name may be there for ever: and mine eyes and mine heart shall be there perpetually."
2 Chronicles 7:12-16

"…and their prayer came up to his holy dwelling place, even unto heaven." 2 Chronicles 30:27

"Let thine ear now be attentive, and thine eyes open, that thou mayest hear the prayer of thy servant, which I pray … and confess the sins of the children of Israel, which we have sinned against thee: *both I and my father's house have sinned."* Nehemiah 1:6

"O Lord, I beseech thee, let now thine ear be attentive to the prayer of thy servant, and to the prayer of thy servants, who desire to fear thy name: and prosper," Nehemiah 1:11

"When my soul fainted within me I remembered the LORD: and my prayer came in unto thee, into thine holy temple." Jonah 2:7

"Nevertheless **we made our prayer unto our God**, and set a watch against them day and night, because of them." Nehemiah 4:9

"…to begin the thanksgiving in prayer:" Nehemiah 11:17

"…also my **prayer is pure**…" Job 16:17

"Thou shalt make thy prayer unto him, and he shall hear thee, and thou shalt pay thy vows." Job 22:27

*"My voice shalt thou **hear in the morning, O LORD; in the morning will I direct my prayer unto thee, and will look up**."* Psalms 5:3

*"Hear the right, O LORD, attend unto my cry, give ear unto my prayer, **that goeth not out of feigned lips**."* Psalms 17:1

*"Yet the LORD will command his lovingkindness in the daytime, and in the night his song shall be with me, **and my prayer unto the God of my life.**"* Psalms 42:8

Identification with God.

"His name shall endure for ever: his name shall be continued as long as the sun: and men shall be blessed in him: all nations shall call him blessed. Blessed be the LORD God, the God of Israel, who only doeth wondrous things. And blessed be his glorious name for ever: and let the whole earth be filled with his glory; Amen, and Amen." Psalms 72:17-20

Psalm 72 is a Psalm of exaltation, declaring the works of our God and magnifying His name. It comes to an end with the words -The prayers of David the son of Jesse are ended.

*"… **when ye make many prayers**, I will not hear: **your hands are full of blood.**"* Isaiah 1:15

*"**Praying always with all prayer and supplication in the Spirit, and watching thereunto with all perseverance and supplication for all saints;**"* Ephesians 6:18

*"**Be careful for nothing; but in every thing by prayer and supplication with thanksgiving let your requests be made known unto God.**"* Philippians 4:6

"These all continued with one accord in prayer and supplication, with the women, and Mary the mother of Jesus, and with his brethren."
Acts 1:14

"And I will pour upon the house of David, and upon the inhabitants of Jerusalem, the spirit of grace and of supplications:" Zechariah 12:10

"If thou wouldest seek unto God betimes, and make thy supplication to the Almighty; If thou wert pure and upright; surely now he would awake for thee, and make the habitation of thy righteousness prosperous. Though thy beginning was small, yet thy latter end should greatly increase." Job 8:5-7

Chapter Sixteen
The Menace Of The Prophetic Hounds

There is a promise of a prophetic generation and before they would arise, the false prophetic scoundrels and hounds have invaded the land. Africa seems to be the worst hit by these pseudo miracle workers and false prophets. Ghana seems to be the origin of the false prophets in Africa and Nigeria has since engulfed every other nation with this brand.

Dr. Emeka Ozurumba of Today Evangelical Ministries, has questioned the authenticity of genuine salvation among ministers and in the churches, especially in Nigeria.

I recently came across Dr. Sunday Adelaja, who has been crying out against idolatry in Nigerian churches.

In recent times, a young man Jay Israel, who once prophesied by Baal, has been exposing prophetic charlatans.

There are two branches of these hounds. The one that prophesy by Baal and Jezebel, using marine-witchcraft and the occult and the ones that prophesy by Google, Facebook and paid actors.

America started it all, from decades ago using electronic devices to get information and prophesy. These are the impersonators that William Marion Branham spoke about.

One prophetic hound in Johannesburg, South Africa almost fooled me. I thought he was a Sniper, having amazing and detailed words of knowledge. He speaks about his pedigree and how as an intercessor he spends eighteen hours on his knees in prayers. Very convincing!!!

What did not add up was, there were no calls for salvation.

South Africans like a few tribes in Nigeria, and maybe other African tribes, mix Christianity with voodoo practices. Some people he prophesied to, had gone to Sangomas (South African witch doctors); and there were no prayers for repentance and for salvation. Quite amazing!!!

One of their new deceptions, to try and legitimize themselves is to become sons to some preachers who appear reputable, especially from Nigeria. I will go into details about these hounds and superstar Pastors, in my soon to be released book YHVH's RoadMap. This book will show you how your prophetic destinies have been hijacked and how you can take them back from this present church system.

Many people have been battered by these prophetic hounds that arrange miracles and prophecies using paid actors. I want to assure you that there is the genuine prophetic and a prophet and prophetic generation will soon be made manifest who will glorify God. They will pay the price through consecration and their words will not fail nor fall to the ground as it was with Moses and Samuel and they will be characterized by love and meekness. This is your invitation to enroll in the Holy Ghost Invasion Sniper Corps and be a genuine Sniper.

I pray for the healing of the memories for those who have been wounded and spent thousands of dollars traveling to such places.

The Bible is the more sure word of prophecy.

"We have also a more sure word of prophecy; whereunto ye do well that ye take heed, as unto a light that shineth in a dark place, until the day dawn, and the day star arise in your hearts:" 2 Peter 1:19

Christianity 101 is -- "My sheep, hear my voice."

"My sheep hear my voice, and I know them, and they follow me:" John 10:27

Does He know you? Be a Sniper today!!!

CHAPTER Seventeen
The Power of Sacrifice

And when the king of Moab saw that the battle was too sore for him, he took with him seven hundred men that drew swords, to break through even unto the king of Edom: but they could not.

Then he took his eldest son that should have reigned in his stead, and offered him for a burnt offering upon the wall. And there was great indignation against Israel: and they departed from him, and returned to their own land. II Ki 3:26-27

If the sacrifice of a heathen king brought such a great salvation to himself, the rest of his family and to his nation; What effect will the sacrifice of Jehovah produce in our lives, when He sacrificed His only begotten son on our behalf?

But this man, after he had offered one sacrifice for sins forever, sat down on the right hand of God;
From henceforth expecting till his enemies be made his footstool.
Heb. 10:12-13

The great YeHoVaH God is waiting for His Navy SEALs to fulfill purpose - *expecting His enemies be made His footstool.*

Without counsel purposes are disappointed: but in the multitude of counsellors they are established. Proverbs 15:22

Without a script,(thoughts, imaginations) to direct, produce and act out your purpose, divine destiny is aborted. However, when you tend the word and sharpen your hearing and apply your thoughts and imaginations using The Script(ures), your destiny movie is established. EFOV

The scripture tells us that "as a man thinketh, so is he" Proverbs 23:7

My days are past, my purposes *are broken off, even the thoughts of my heart.*
Job 17:11

The things which I greatly feared came upon me. Job 3:25

Job was afraid and began to think and paint pictures, making a movie from the devil's script. Up and until this chapter and further more, his thought were warped. However, the little string or glimmer of hope was his trust in God. He persevered to the end.

Being confident of this very thing, that he which hath begun a good work in you will perform it until the day of Jesus Christ: Philippians 1:6

We can see in the life of Job the making of a Navy SEAL.

I Cannot Afford To Quit

Quite a few make it through the initial qualification assessment as a Navy SEAL, but when the goings get tough many quit. It is said about 25% graduate. All it takes to quit is to ring the bell three times and doff your helmet. You donned your helmet to begin the race to become a Navy SEAL, but those who will not continue bow out. They bowed down to the overwhelming circumstance.

Circumstances have a voice, but how you react or respond to it, is what puts you under or over. Jesus Christ had walked to a fig tree, hungry and desiring a fruit from it but the fig tree spoke to Jesus. How many times have your empty refrigerator, pocket or bank account spoken to you? It tells you it is a hopeless situation, you and your children are going to go to bed with an empty stomach, you are going to lose your house etc.

I strongly believe that those who quit, reacted and bowed down to circumstances and those who overcame responded to the circumstances.

And seeing a fig tree afar off having leaves, he came, if haply he might find any thing thereon: and when he came to it, he found nothing but leaves; for the time of figs was not yet.

And Jesus answered and said unto it, No man eat fruit of thee hereafter for ever. And his disciples heard it. Mark 11:13-14

And in the morning, as they passed by, they saw the fig tree dried up from the roots.

And Peter calling to remembrance saith unto him, Master, behold, the fig tree which thou cursedst is withered away. Mark 11:20-21

Jesus answered and said unto them, Verily I say unto you, If ye have faith, and doubt not, ye shall not only do this which is done to the fig tree, but also if ye shall say unto this mountain, Be thou removed, and be thou cast into the sea; it shall be done.

And all things, whatsoever ye shall ask in prayer, believing, ye shall receive.

Matthew 21:21-22

Here, we see our Lord Jesus Christ answered the tree. He answered the circumstance that faced Him. He spoke to it. I do not know what made the overcoming SEALs not to quit but I would think this everlasting principle worked for them. They spoke to the prevailing circumstance. *"I cannot and will not quit,*

I will not fail my team. Circumstance, I say unto you, wither in Jesus Name Amen"

I wish we could dissect the minds of them that make it and ask how they made it.

In another situation, Jesus was in the boat with His disciples and a circumstance arose.

And there arose a great storm of wind, and the waves beat into the ship, so that it was now full.

And he was in the hinder part of the ship, asleep on a pillow: and they awake him, and say unto him, Master, carest thou not that we perish?

And he arose, and rebuked the wind, and said unto the sea, Peace, be still. And the wind ceased, and there was a great calm.

And he said unto them, Why are ye so fearful? how is it that ye have no faith?

Mark 4:37-40

Does fear assail the Navy SEAL? Yes! Are there times they would have given up? Yes!

These are men who have chosen to walk on the water and many times, contrary winds or boisterous waves are working against them.

And straightway he constrained his disciples to get into the ship, and to go to the other side before unto Bethsaida, while he sent away the people.

And when he had sent them away, he departed into a mountain to pray.

And when even was come, the ship was in the midst of the sea, and he alone on the land.

And he saw them toiling in rowing; for the wind was contrary unto them: and about the fourth watch of the night he cometh unto them, walking upon the sea, and would have passed by them.

But when they saw him walking upon the sea, they supposed it had been a spirit, and cried out:

For they all saw him, and were troubled. And immediately he talked with them, and saith unto them, Be of good cheer: it is I; be not afraid.

And he went up unto them into the ship; and the wind ceased: and they were sore amazed in themselves beyond measure, and wondered. Mark 6:45-51

In the Matthew version of the same story, the account of Peter walking on the water was added.

And Peter answered him and said, Lord, if it be thou, bid me come unto thee on the water.

And he said, Come. And when Peter was come down out of the ship, he walked on the water, to go to Jesus.

But when he saw the wind boisterous, he was afraid; and beginning to sink, he cried, saying, Lord, save me.

And immediately Jesus stretched forth his hand, and caught him, and said unto him, O thou of little faith, wherefore didst thou doubt?

And when they were come into the ship, the wind ceased. Matthew 14:28- 32

I would want to believe that like Peter, many times they have cried unto the LORD, help us, you did not bring us this far to abandon us.

The Navy SEALs have rowed the boat, contesting with waves, storms and winds; with weariness and sleep deprivation but they made it to the shores.

The Apostle Paul spoke about those who contend in the Olympics to win a bouquet of flowers and today gold, silver and bronze medals.

Know ye not that they which run in a race run all, but one receiveth the prize? So run, that ye may obtain.

And every man that striveth for the mastery is temperate in all things. Now they do it to obtain a corruptible crown; but we an incorruptible.

I therefore so run, not as uncertainly; so fight I, not as one that beateth the air:

But I keep under my body, and bring it into subjection: lest that by any means, when I have preached to others, I myself should be a castaway. 1 Corinthians 9:24-27

The Trident Pin is for those that endure to the end against all odds.

Here we are talking about God's gallant and overcoming armies or Navy SEALs.

In the book of Revelations chapters 2 and 3, we see this phrase over and over again

"*To him that overcometh...*" ; and the accompanying rewards.

These were present fears and real dangers but they made it to the end.

Job was a Navy SEAL who went through great testings and trials. He was confronted on every sides. His primary issues were the things he feared. The wife pressurized him to give up, his friends were of no help, his confessions were not good. Only one string of hope in his statement: --I know my redeemer liveth.

One day I came across the very uplifting song by Nicole C. Mullen, "My Redeemer Lives" sung with an angelic voice. "... Whose words alone can catch a falling star? ... My redeemer lives.... Because He lives I can face tomorrow.... He conquered death and gave me the victory... He lives to take away my shame..."

He took away my shame of wanting to quit and gave me the victory. One very important thing we must know as God's Navy

SEALs is that He conquered death and gave us the victory. At the end of it all Job had the victory and was blessed beyond measure.

Joseph had a dream of ruling someday. As a Navy SEAL, he was confronted by household wickedness, thrown into a pit, sold into slavery and ended up in prison. Through it all, he refused to defile himself because his allegiance was to God. At the end of it all, he received his Trident Pin and crown.

David went through thick and thin but at the end he became king of Judah and finally of all Israel. It pays to hold on unto the end.

Jesus overcame! His eyes was on the prize.

Looking unto Jesus the author and finisher of our faith; who for the joy that was set before him endured the cross, despising the shame, and is set down at the right hand of the throne of God.

For consider him that endured such contradiction of sinners against himself, lest ye be wearied and faint in your minds. Hebrews 12:2-3 (Proverbs 3:11-12)

An Expected End

For I know the thoughts that I think toward you, saith the LORD, thoughts of peace, and not of evil, to give you an expected end. Jeremiah 29:11

We know the end of the story, we win. One thing that we must always acknowledge is that we are created in the image and likeness of God

And God said, Let us make man in our image, after our likeness: and let them have dominion over the fish of the sea, and over the fowl of the air, and over the cattle, and over all the earth, and over every creeping thing that creepeth upon the earth.

So God created man in his own image, in the image of God created

he him; male and female created he them.

And God blessed them, and God said unto them, Be fruitful, and multiply, and replenish the earth, and subdue it: and have dominion *over the fish of the sea, and over the fowl of the air, and over every living thing that moveth upon the earth.*

Genesis 1:26-28

Since you are created in the image and likeness of God, It would be appropriate to declare:

"You will never know who you are, until you know who God Is."

Subdue will imply that there are some opposing forces that must be brought under subjection.

Replenish would imply power to revitalize that which has been depleted.

Dominion would imply to exert authority and power to reign in life

No Identity, No Purpose

John the Baptist was able to identify himself as the voice crying in the wilderness.

Jesus knew His identity and purpose. John called Him the Lamb of God, Peter said "*Thou art the Christ the Son of the living God* "

His personal testimony:

The Spirit of the Lord is upon me, because he hath anointed me to preach the gospel to the poor; he hath sent me to heal the brokenhearted, to preach deliverance to the captives, and recovering

of sight to the blind, to set at liberty them that are bruised,
   Luke 4:18

Looking unto Jesus the author and finisher of our faith; who for the joy that was set before him endured the cross, despising the shame, and is set down at the right hand of the throne of God. Hebrews 12:2

We are destined as overcomers to the throne of God just like Jesus our Elder brother.

To him that overcometh will I grant to sit with me in my throne, even as I also overcame, and am set down with my Father in his throne. Revelations 3:21

Apostle Paul knew his identity.

But rise, and stand upon thy feet: for *I have appeared unto thee* for this purpose, *to make thee a minister and a witness both of these things which thou hast seen, and of those things in the which I will appear unto thee;* Acts 26:16

Apostle Paul identified himself as the Apostle to the Gentiles and understood his purpose.and fulfilled it. He declared:

But what things were gain to me, those I counted loss for Christ.
Yea doubtless, and I count all things but loss for the excellency of the knowledge of Christ Jesus my Lord: for whom I have suffered the loss of all things, and do count them but dung, that I may win Christ,
And be found in him, not having mine own righteousness, which is of the law, but that which is through the faith of Christ, the righteousness which is of God by faith:
That I may know him, and the power of his resurrection, and the fellowship of his sufferings, being made conformable unto his

death;

If by any means I might attain unto the resurrection of the dead.

Not as though I had already attained, either were already perfect: but I follow after, if that I may apprehend that for which also I am apprehended of Christ Jesus.

Brethren, I count not myself to have apprehended: but this one thing I do, forgetting those things which are behind, and reaching forth unto those things which are before,

I press toward the mark for the prize of the high calling of God in Christ Jesus.

Philippians 3:7-14

For I am now ready to be offered, and the time of my departure is at hand.

I have fought a good fight, I have finished my course, I have kept the faith:

Henceforth there is laid up for me a crown of righteousness, which the Lord, the righteous judge, shall give me at that day: and not to me only, but unto all them also that love his appearing. 2 Timothy 4:6-8

Until then, no dungeons, no Sharks, Whales, Sea , Wild animals, Viper nor Nero could take him out.

It is important to know that we are called according to His purpose, called to be like Jesus Christ. Romans 8:28-29.

We are called by His Name and His SEAL is upon us and we have the ministry of angels, as a result we cannot quit.

And now thy two sons, Ephraim and Manasseh, which were born unto thee in the land of Egypt before I came unto thee into Egypt, are mine; as Reuben and Simeon, they shall be mine.

And thy issue, which thou begettest after them, shall be thine, and shall be called after the name of their brethren in their inheritance.

...The Angel which redeemed me from all evil, bless the lads; and let

my name be named on them, and the name of my fathers Abraham and Isaac; and let them grow into a multitude in the midst of the earth. Genesis 48:5-6,16

Here we see Ephraim and Manasseh being made sons of Jacob, having inheritance in Jacob as Joseph their father and thus Joseph becomes their elder brother. God the Father did the same for us

And if children, then heirs; heirs of God, and joint-heirs with Christ; if so be that we suffer with him, that we may be also glorified together. Romans 8:17

Are they not all ministering spirits, sent forth to minister for them who shall be heirs of salvation? Hebrews 1:14

Wherein God, willing more abundantly to shew unto the heirs of *promise the immutability* of *his counsel, confirmed it by an oath*: Hebrews 6:17

Hearken, my beloved brethren, Hath not God chosen the poor of *this world rich in faith, and* heirs of *the kingdom which he hath promised to them that love him?* James 2:5

For the promise, that he should be the heir of the world, was not to Abraham, or to his seed, through the law, but through the righteousness of faith.
For if they which are of the law be heirs, faith is made void, and the promise made of none effect: Romans 4:13-14

That being justified by his grace, we should be made heirs according to the hope of eternal life. Titus 3:7

Likewise, ye husbands, dwell with them according to knowledge, giving honour unto the wife, as unto the weaker vessel, and as being heirs together of the grace of life; that your prayers be not hindered. 1 Peter 3:7

My beloved brethren, with these overwhelming testimonies of scriptures, you cannot and must not quit. Many are counting on you. I am counting on you as being heirs together.

In the evil days ahead, through the waters, through the fire, in the lions den, or in the dungeons of this world, we will not bow, bend or break. Our resolve is absolute, we are being purified like silver and gold to remove every dross. The fourth man appears in the crucible of affliction. We will arise an smite with plagues as Moses in Egypt and call down fire like Elijah and the world will know that YeHoVaH has His Navy SEALs. The power of the age to come will be manifested by YHVH's Navy SEALs

CHAPTER Eighteen
The Key Of David

And to the angel of the church in Philadelphia write; These things saith he that is holy, he that is true, he that hath the key of David, he that openeth, and no man shutteth; and shutteth, and no man openeth; Revelations 3:7 (Isaiah 22:22)

This key, in the hands of the authorized ones will unlock things that have never being seen in the annals of history. This is the power of the age to come

For unto us a child is born, unto us a son is given: and the government shall be upon his shoulder: and his name shall be called Wonderful, Counsellor, The mighty God, The everlasting Father, The Prince of Peace.
Of the increase of his government and peace there shall be no end, upon the throne of David, and upon his kingdom, to order it, and to establish it with judgment and with justice from henceforth even for ever. The zeal of the LORD of hosts will perform this.
Isaiah 9:6-7

This is a governmental key of authority and power, not only belonging to Jesus Christ but to His Seed.

Behold, I and the children whom the LORD hath given me are for signs and for wonders in Israel from the LORD of hosts, which dwelleth in mount Zion. Isaiah 8:18.

The Spirit of the Lord GOD is upon me; because the LORD hath anointed me to preach good tidings unto the meek; he hath sent me to bind up the brokenhearted, to proclaim liberty to the captives, and the opening of the prison to them that are bound;

To proclaim the acceptable year of the LORD, and the day of vengeance of our God; to comfort all that mourn; Isaiah 61:1-2

Jesus Christ read from this scroll in Isaiah as we see in Luke 4:18; however, he left out the second part of verse 2 - and the day of vengeance of our God; to comfort all that mourn.

There is work to be done by YHVH's Navy SEALs as heirs of the world.

Thou shalt break them with a rod of iron; thou shalt dash them in pieces like a potter's vessel. Psalms 2:9

And he shall rule them with a rod of iron; as the vessels of a potter shall they be broken to shivers: even as I received of my Father. Revelations 2:27

And she brought forth a man child, who was to rule all nations with a rod of iron: and her child was caught up unto God, and to his throne. Revelations 12:15

And out of his mouth goeth a sharp sword, that with it he should smite the nations: and he shall rule them with a rod of iron: and he treadeth the winepress of the fierceness and wrath of Almighty God. Revelations 19:15

A very pertinent question was asked in Isaiah 53:8, after the initial question in verse 1

Who hath believed our report? and to whom is the arm of the

LORD revealed?

For he shall grow up before him as a tender plant, and as a root out of a dry ground: he hath no form nor comeliness; and when we shall see him, there is no beauty that we should desire him.

He is despised and rejected of men; a man of sorrows, and acquainted with grief: and we hid as it were our faces from him; he was despised, and we esteemed him not.

Surely he hath borne our griefs, and carried our sorrows: yet we did esteem him stricken, smitten of God, and afflicted.

But he was wounded for our transgressions, he was bruised for our iniquities: the chastisement of our peace was upon him; and with his stripes we are healed.

All we like sheep have gone astray; we have turned every one to his own way; and the LORD hath laid on him the iniquity of us all.

He was oppressed, and he was afflicted, yet he opened not his mouth: he is brought as a lamb to the slaughter, and as a sheep before her shearers is dumb, so he openeth not his mouth.

He was taken from prison and from judgment: and who shall declare his generation? *for he was cut off out of the land of the living: for the transgression of my people was he stricken.*

And he made his grave with the wicked, and with the rich in his death; because he had done no violence, neither was any deceit in his mouth.

Yet it pleased the LORD to bruise him; he hath put him to grief: *when thou shalt make his soul an offering for sin,* he shall see his seed, he shall prolong his days, and the pleasure of the LORD shall prosper in his hand.

He shall see of the travail of his soul, and shall be satisfied: by his knowledge shall my righteous servant justify many; for he shall bear their iniquities.

Therefore will I divide him a portion with the great, and he shall divide the spoil with the strong; because he hath poured out his soul unto death: and he was numbered with the transgressors; and he bare the sin of many, and made intercession for the transgressors.

We are the travail of His Soul; we are His Seed and are for signs and wonders. He has been waiting for two Millenniums to unveil His masterpiece.

The Gathering Clouds And Oncoming Storm

Why do the heathen rage, and the people imagine a vain thing?

The kings of the earth set themselves, and the rulers take counsel together, against the LORD, and against his anointed, saying,

Let us break their bands asunder, and cast away their cords from us.

He that sitteth in the heavens shall laugh: the Lord shall have them in derision.

Then shall he speak unto them in his wrath, and vex them in his sore displeasure.

Yet have I set my king upon my holy hill of Zion.

I will declare the decree: the LORD hath said unto me, Thou art my Son; this day have I begotten thee.

Ask of me, and I shall give thee the heathen for thine inheritance, and the uttermost parts of the earth for thy possession.

Thou shalt break them with a rod of iron; thou shalt dash them in pieces like a potter's vessel.

Be wise now therefore, O ye kings: be instructed, ye judges of the earth.

Serve the LORD with fear, and rejoice with trembling.

Kiss the Son, lest he be angry, and ye perish from the way, when his wrath is kindled but a little. Blessed are all they that put their trust in him. Psalms 2:1-12

Israel is YHVH's time piece, Jerusalem is the eternal capital of God, yet the heathen have contested with God. The Arabs and the United Nations have contested Jerusalem with the children of Israel. America vowed to stand with Israel. The nation of Israel declared Jerusalem as their Capital in 1950, in 1967 annexed the Eastern half that was under the control of Jordan in the Six Day

War. The rest of the world would not agree with them and had their embassies in Tel-Aviv.

President Barack Hussenni Obama vetoed the move of the American Embassy to Jerusalem. However, a President with guts, President Donald J Trump, did what was said to be impossible by moving the United States Embassy to Jerusalem.

In the 8 years tenure of President Obama, his policy deliberately decimated the USA Army to lay the ground work for Globalist take over and usher in the Antichrist. He also created a vacuum in the Middle East which Russia filled by moving into Syria. Three major players - Russia, Iran and Turkey are presently in Syria next door to Israel, and some day very soon The Red Army will also make their move across the Euphrates river.

The Blue States, the Deep State and the Globalists along with the World Council of Churches are grievously working against the Christ.

This is what Psalms 2 is talking about, but YHVH has His Sons, His Navy SEALs with the rod of Iron.

There are important visions of America that are pertinent here. One was given by Evangelist A. A Allen -- Vision of the Destruction of America, which is a good read. There is also one by various men of God past and present of the splitting of America in two halves from the fault line in Missouri, if they divide Israel. I was in a meeting in August 10th of 2016, when a Prophet of God said he saw Donald J Trump in the Council of Heaven and that he was going to be the next President of the United States of America. He said President J Trump was going to be a Cyrus. He has made things happen like no other President in history and more is yet to come.

It is quite amazing that no President in history has ever been so vilified, harassed and hated by the whole world. World powers, nations, the Democrats and the American mainline media, whom he rightly tagged the Fake News Media. The coming of President Obama was greeted by the whole world and that is how the Antichrist will be ushered in. The stage is being set and it is under these circumstances, the Sons of God must arise, God's Navy SEALs and Snippers at the End time.

In the 2016 election, we were on the verge of two prophetic timelines meeting, but YHVH intervened. We will see these in the vision given to William Marion Branham.

The 1933 Vision by William Marion Branham

1.   The first vision was that Mussolini would invade Ethiopia and that nation would "fall at his steps." That vision surely did cause some repercussions, and some were very angry when I said it and would not believe it. But it happened that way. He just walked in there with his modern arms and took over. The natives didn't have a chance. But the vision also said that Mussolini would come to a horrible end with his own people turning on him. That came to pass just exactly as it was said.

2.   The next vision foretold that an Austrian by the name of Adolph Hitler would rise up as dictator over Germany, and that he would draw the world into war. It showed the Siegfried line and how our troops would have a terrible time to overcome it. Then it showed that Hitler would come to a mysterious end.

3.   The third vision was in the realm of world politics for it showed me that there would be three great ISMS, Facism, Nazism, Communism, but that the first two would be swallowed up into the third. The voice admonished, "WATCH RUSSIA, WATCH RUSSIA. Keep your eye on the King of the North."

4.   The fourth vision showed the great advances in science that would come after the second world war. It was headed up in the vision of a plastic bubble-topped car that was running down beautiful highways under remote control so that people appeared seated in this car without a steering wheel and they were playing some sort of a game to amuse themselves.

5.   The fifth vision had to do with the moral problem of our age, centering mostly around women. God showed me that women began to be out of their place with the granting of the vote. Then

they cut off their hair, which signified that they were no longer under the authority of a man but insisted on either equal rights, or in most cases, more than equal rights. She adopted men's clothing and went into a state of undress, until the last picture I saw was a woman naked except for a little fig leaf type apron. With this vision I saw the terrible perversion and moral plight of the whole world.

6. Then in the sixth vision there arose up in America a most beautiful, but cruel woman. She held the people in her complete power. I believed that this was the rise of the Roman Catholic Church, though I knew it could possibly be a vision of some woman rising in great power in America due to a popular vote by women.

7. The last and seventh vision was wherein I heard a most terrible explosion. As I turned to look I saw nothing but debris, craters, and smoke all over the land of America.

William Marion Branham, June 1933 (Voice of God Recordings)

Visions 1, 2 and 3 have happened to the letter, while Vision 5 has been playing out before our eyes for decades. I was in South Africa a few years ago and saw a horrible site. A lady wore a dress with the back cleavage hanging out and the front was skimpily covered.

The decadence is unparalleled in modern history. An Uber driver told me such is common here in Conservative Phoenix Arizona, and you can only imagine what obtains in California and New York. William Branham once said "If God does not judge California, he would have to apologize to Sodom and Gomorrah".

Vision 4 is also playing out before our eyes. We have seen the changes in car designs since 1933 until now. Cars are oval shape. Visions 4 and 6 almost played out in 2016 with Google going to usher in the Driverless Car and Hillary Clinton breaking the glass ceiling.

It was not to be, because grace was extended to us by the coming of President J Trump.

Cadillac Super Cruise seems to be leading in the innovation of the driverless cars and many are on the heels of this great innovations.

All that is needed now is a superhighway or how to adapt to the present highway grid.

With the most fraudulent election in American history we are at the verge of the two visions coming together again.

If God is merciful to America and thus the world, we will have another four years of grace.

The Globalist have taken over Europe. Europe is already fallen! All that is left is for Tanks to roll out all over Europe according to a vision I saw over a decade ago. Trumps America, is a stumbling block. Americans having guns will create some problems and that is why the agenda of the Left is to take away their Second Amendment Rights and make the people vulnerable. The coming of the beautiful and wicked woman will be disguised subtilely but it shall surely come to pass. After which, great destruction comes to America according to Vision 7.

It is in such dark climate that YHVH's Navy SEALs and End time Snipers have great roles to play to establish the Kingdom of God on the earth.

Over a decade ago, I had a dream, one of the USS Carriers was in the Gulf near Galveston, Texas. I saw this massive Carrier like a whole village. Many were dressed going to the ballrooms, some to the movie theaters while others were moving aimlessly.

In my spirit I saw missiles coming from the Pacific Ocean and there was no response from this Carrier. I ran to raise the alarm and to enlist to fight the enemies but they were docile and unresponsive.

The Democrats, with their Leftist agenda and as in the 8 years of President Obama will cause our military to be docile. They will sell America to the Globalist and betray Israel and judgment will surely come upon the land of the free and brave. However, there is hope; for there is the Remnant Church, who like the three Hebrew children, will not bow to the image of the Beast. These Holy Ghost Navy SEALs and Snipers were born for such a time as this.

Arise, shine; for thy light is come, and the glory of the LORD is risen upon thee.

For, behold, the darkness shall cover the earth, and gross darkness the people: but the LORD shall arise upon thee, and his glory shall be seen upon thee.

And the Gentiles shall come to thy light, and kings to the brightness of thy rising.

Isaiah 60:1-3

The 1679 Prophecy by Jane Leade, talks about this Remnant and Virgin Church and the Key of David.

1679 Prophecy By: Jane Leade

There shall be a total and full redemption by Christ. This is a hidden mystery not to be understood without the revelation of the Holy Spirit. The Holy Spirit is at hand to reveal the same to all holy seekers and loving inquirers. The completion of such a redemption is withheld and abstracted by the apocalyptical (or revelation) seals.

Wherefore as the Spirit of God shall open up seal after seal, so shall this redemption come to be revealed both particularly and universally. In the gradual opening of the mystery of redemption in Christ doth consist the unsearchable wisdom of God; which may continually reveal new and fresh things to the worthy seeker. In order to which the ark of the Testimony in Heaven shall be opened before the end of this age and the living testimony herein contained shall be unsealed. The presence of the Divine Ark will constitute the life of this

Virgin Church, and wherever this body is, there must the ark of necessity be.

The unsealing of the Living Testimony within the Ark of God must begin the promulgation of the everlasting gospel of the kingdom. The proclamation of the Testimony will be as the sounding of a trumpet of alarm to the nations of professed Christendom. Authority shall be given by Christ to the putting an end to all controversies concerning the true church that is born of the New Jerusalem mother. This decision will be the actual sealing of the body of Christ with the name (or Authority) of God, giving them a commission to act by the same.

This New Name (or Authority) will distinguish them from the seven thousand names of Babylon. The election and preparation of this Virgin Church is to be after a secret and hidden manner. As David in his ministry was chosen and anointed by the prophet of the Lord, yet was not admitted to the outward profession of the Kingdom for a considerable time afterward, of the stem of David a Virgin Church, which hath known nothing of a man or human constitution, is to be born and it will require some time for it to get out of the minority and arrive at full and mature age.

The birth of this Virgin Church was typified by St. John's vision where the great wonder appeared in heaven, bringing forth her first born that was caught up to the throne of God (or identified with the Authority of God). For as a virgin woman brought forth Christ after the flesh, so shall a Virgin Church bring forth the first born after the Spirit who shall be endowed with the seven spirits of God. This church so brought forth and sealed with the mark of Divine Authority will have no bonds or impositions, but the holy unction among these new born spirits will be all and all.

There is not at this day (1679) visible upon the earth such a church, all profession being found light when weighed in the balances. Therefore they are rejected by the Supreme Judge. Which rejection will be for this cause, that out of them may come a new and glorious church. Then shall the glory of God and the Lamb so rest upon this typical tabernacle so that it shall be called the Tabernacle of Wisdom, and though it is not now known in visibility, yet it shall be seen as coming out of the wilderness within a short time; then it will go on to

multiply and propagate itself universally, not only to the number of the first born (144,000) but also to the remnant of the seed, against whom the Dragon will make war continually.

Wherefore the spirit of David shall revive in this blossoming root. These will have might given them to overcome the Dragon and his angels, even as David overcame Goliath and the Philistine army. This will be the standing up of the great prince Michael and will be as the appearance of Moses against Pharaoh, in order that the chosen seed may be brought out of hard servitude.

Egypt doth figure this servile creation under which Abraham's seed groans, but a prophet, and the most prophetical generation, will the Most High raise up who shall deliver His people by the force of spiritual arms.

For which there must be certain head powers to bear the first office, who are to be persons in favor with God, whose dread and fear shall fall on all nations, visible and invisible, because of the mighty acting power of the Holy Spirit which shall rest upon them. For Christ will appear in some chosen vessels to bring into the Promised Land, the New Creation state.

Thus, Moses, Joshua, and Aaron may be considered types of some upon whom the same Spirit will come, yet in greater proportion. Whereby they shall make way for the ransomed of the Lord to return to Mt. Zion, but none shall stand under God but those who have become "tried" stones after the pattern and similitude of Christ. This will be fiery trial through which a very few will be able to pass or bear up in it. Whereby the waiters for this visible breaking forth are strictly charged to hold fast, and wait together in the unity of Pure Love. This

trial will be of absolute necessity to all for the clearing away of all remaining infirmities of the natural mind, and the burning of all hay, wood, and stubble. For nothing must remain in the fire, for as a refiner shall He purify the

sons of the kingdom.

There will be some who will be fully redeemed being clothed upon with a priestly garment after the Melchizedek order. This will qualify them for governing Authority. Therefore it is required on their part to suffer the Spirit of burning, and the fanning of the Fiery Breath searching every part within them until they arrive at a Fixed Body from whence the wonders are to flow out.

Upon this body will be the fixation of the Urim and Thummim that are the portion of the Melchizedek priesthood whose descent is not counted in the genealogy of that creation which is under the fall but in another genealogy

which is a New Creation. Hence these priests will have a deep inward search and divine sight into secret things of Deity, will be able to prophesy in a clear ground; not darkly and enigmatically, for they will know what is couched in the first originality of all beings, in the eternal anti-type of nature, and will be able to bring them forth according to the divine counsel and ordination.

The Lord sweareth in truth and righteousness that from Abraham's line, according to the Spirit, there shall arise a Holy Priesthood. Abraham and Sarah were a type of that which would be produced and manifested in the last age. The mighty Spirit of Cyrus is appointed to lay the foundation of this third temple and support it in the building.

There are characteristics and marks whereby the pure Virgin Church shall be known and distinguished from all others and whereby the unction and true sound of the Holy Spirit shall be discerned from all others that are low, false and counterfeit. There must be a manifestation of the Spirit whereby to edify and raise up this Church, whereby bringing heaven down upon the earth and representing here the New Jerusalem state in order to which spirits are thus begotten and born of God, ascend to New Jerusalem above where their Head in majesty doth reign.

None but those who have so ascended and received of His glory can condescend and communicate the same, being thereby His representatives on the earth and subordinate priests under Him now. He that has ascended and glorified has made Himself, as it were, our Debtor. Consequently, He will not be wanting in qualifying and furnishing certain high and principal instruments who shall be most humble and as little regarded as David was, who He will dignify with honor and priestly sovereignty for drawing to them the scattered flocks and gathering them into one fold out of all nations.

Therefore, there should be a holy emulation and ambition stirred up among the bands of believers that they may be of the firstfruits unto Him that is risen from the dead and so be made principal agents for Him and with Him, that they may be, if possible, of the number of the First-born, of the New Jerusalem mother. All true waiters of His Kingdom in Spirit, under whatsoever profession they may be, ought to be numbered among the virgin spirits to whom this message appertains. Be watchful and quicken your pace." By permission from A Good Report By A Heavenly Spy, Larry Hodges

The Key of David will be in the hands of this Virgin Church and they can shut whole Cities and neighborhoods from the Antichrist and label them Cities of Refuge.
They would go to the Antichrist Camp and drive away food trucks to Cities and Neighborhoods of Refuge. They will multiply

food like Jesus and Elijah. They are able to move in stealth mode and are able to appear and disappear at will. They will cause grievous damage to the Antichrist supply lines, take down radars, installations and Generals. The world has never seen the likes of these before. They shall defeat the Antichrist and false prophets and the world will know that Jesus has a Seed and the kingdom of this world shall be the kingdom of Christ and His Seed.

And to the angel of the church in Philadelphia write; These things saith he that is holy, he that is true, he that hath the key of David, he that openeth, and no man shutteth; and shutteth, and no man openeth; Revelations 3:7 (Isaiah 22:22)

Enroll today in the Holy Ghost Invasion Sniper School and Navy SEALs training and let us fulfill the Genesis mandate to subdue the earth, replenish it and have dominion.

Christ is our Anchor and Ark of safety in this on coming storm!!!

Epilogue

Dear child of God, there is still so much to write on this subject of the Sniper's Prayer: The Gathering of Eagle Saints; The Spirit of David; Travailing Prayers and the Baptism of Fire. However, I must release this book at this time.

We must have genuine conversion and have intimacy with God. Ruth said, *"spread your skirt over me."* My cry is *"Holy Spirit, spread your skirt over us."* We need the baptism of the Holy Spirit, genuine consecration and we also need to know the goal God has set before us.

We cannot neglect the Holy Spirit and His gifts. He is our helper, available to us 24/7 to help us reach fulfillment. It is time to teach more about the Holy Spirit and His gifts in the churches and allow the saints to exercise their gifts. You cannot afford at this time to be constrained by the church you go to as many are blind leaders of the blind. There are good books about the Holy Spirit and His gifts. My favorite is by Harold Horton. Another one is by Lester Sumrall. I will also republish my book on the Holy Spirit titled: Let it Rain.

I beg of you to be proactive with your spiritual life and destiny and reach for the goal God has set for you. Jesus had a goal, so did Paul.

*"…looking unto Jesus, **the** author and finisher of our faith, who for the joy that was set before Him endured the cross, despising the shame, and has sat down at the right hand of the throne of God."* Hebrews 12:2

"I press toward the mark for the prize of the high calling of God in Christ Jesus." Philippians 3:14

God has a goal for you:

"…And to know the love of Christ, which passeth knowledge, that ye might be filled with all the fulness of God." Ephesians 3:19

Do not leave it in the hands of Superstar pastors.
The Covid-19 has kept many away from these churches and now people are realizing that they have to pray for themselves. Do not scuttle your destiny like Gehazi nor warm the pews rooting for and worshiping these pastors.

You are called to the manifestation of the Sons of God and destined for His throne. Arise and be the Sniper God has called you to be.

Be blessed and be a blessing.

www.ingramcontent.com/pod-product-compliance
Lightning Source LLC
Chambersburg PA
CBHW070954190726
48292CB00004B/1452